Charles F. Beezley

Our Social Customs

A practical guide to deportment, easy manners, and social etiquette

Charles F. Beezley

Our Social Customs
A practical guide to deportment, easy manners, and social etiquette

ISBN/EAN: 9783337390532

Printed in Europe, USA, Canada, Australia, Japan

Cover: Foto ©Andreas Hilbeck / pixelio.de

More available books at **www.hansebooks.com**

OUR SOCIAL CUSTOMS.

A PRACTICAL GUIDE TO DEPORTMENT, EASY
MANNERS, AND SOCIAL ETIQUETTE.

BY

DAPHNE DALE.

W. B. CONKEY COMPANY, PUBLISHERS,
CHICAGO, ILL.
1895.

INTRODUCTION.

In a preface the author is privileged to communicate to the public thoughts which do not properly belong in the text of the book. Of this privilege I avail myself.

In naming this volume the same feelings have been with me that come to every mother in choosing a name for her babe. She selects and rejects, again and again, hoping to hit the one most appropriate and pleasing.

I once thought of calling it MY CONFIDENTIAL FRIEND, for such it must become to every reader. This name seemed especially appropriate, for only from a guide like this would we feel, considering our sensitive natures, like accepting advice and hints as plain-spoken as this book contains. No friend, no matter how well-meaning his intentions, could proffer us advice of this nature without causing in us some tinge of resentment. While rejecting this title, I still desire that the book be considered a confidential friend in the sense above stated.

My next impulse was to name the volume " OUR HOME AND ITS CULTURE," for this purpose was uppermost in my mind while preparing it for the public. Many good influences are now being brought to bear, tending to improve and elevate the home and its environments, and to add my mite has been my desire. Dropping this title for the reason that it did not cover all the topics treated of, I selected the one the cover now bears, "*Our Manners and Social Customs.*"   Yet it is amiss in that it smacks too much of cold facts or reminds us of the laws of the statute books, which simply point out the misdemeanors, whereas our aim is to guide to and make it possible for each reader to place himself on the highest plane attained by culture and refinement.

DAPHNE DALE.

CONTENTS.

ORIGIN OF CUSTOMS.. 21
HOME 33
   Influence of Home..................................... 39
   Great Responsibility................................. 39
   Making Home Attractive................................ 40
  DUTIES OF A WIFE.................................... 40
   Owes first Duty to Home.............................. 41
   Strives to Please.................................... 41
   Avoids Confidants.................................... 42
   Practices Economy.................................... 42
   Home Adornments...................................... 43
   Avoids Bickerings.................................... 43
   Commanding Respect................................... 44
  DUTIES OF A HUSBAND.................................. 45
   Self-Control... 45
   Accompanying the Wife to Church...................... 46
   Make a Confidant of the Wife......................... 46
   Do not Interfere with Household Management........... 47
   Words of Encouragement............................... 47
   Be Amiable and Agreeable............................. 48
BOYS... 51
   Classifying Boys..................................... 53
   The Wild Boy... 55
   The Tame Boy... 57
   The Studious Boy..................................... 58
   The Cruel Boy.. 59
   The Eye the Window of the Soul....................... 59
   Be a True Parent to the Boy.......................... 60
   Boys must Battle in Life............................. 62
   Poverty No Barrier................................... 64
GIRLS.. 67
   A Mother's Responsibility............................ 70
   Take your Daughter into your Confidence.............. 72

Chaperons... 73
Teach them Self-reliance.. 73
A Girl's Duty to her Mother and Home...................... 74
Frequently only Ornamental 75
Sterling Worth... 76
COURTSHIP... 79
Choosing a Mate.. 82
Manhood and Womanhood the Basis....................... 83
Married People Meet Adversity Best...................... 84
Choose Judiciously... 85
Be Circumspect... 85
Be not too Hasty 87
Love at first Sight.. 87
The Coquette... 87
Be Frank and Honest... 88
The Rejected Suitor... 89
Do not provoke Lover's Quarrels 90
Proposing... 90
Consulting Her Parents.. 92
The Engagement Ring.. 94
Conduct during Engagement.................................... 94
The Domineering Lover.. 96
Broken Engagements... 96
WEDDINGS... 99
Rites and Ceremonies.. 101
Bridesmaids... 102
Groomsmen 103
Congratulations... 103
Church Weddings... 103
Wedding Cards.. 104
Calling on Newly Wedded Couples.......................... 105
Returning Visits... 105
Additional Hints.. 106
WEDDING ANNIVERSARIES.............................. 109
The Invitations.. 112
The Golden Wedding.. 112
The Gifts Appropriate.. 113
Sometimes Sad.. 113
Silver Wedding.. 114
The Cards and Presents... 114
The Entertainment.. 114
The Crystal Wedding... 115

The Tin Wedding.. 115
The Wooden Wedding...... 115
The Ceremonies, Gifts, etc....... 116
INTRODUCTIONS.. 119
Be sure the introduction is Agreeable......... 123
Host and Hostess Introduce............................. 124
Introductions at Balls.................................... 124
Forms of Introductions.. 124
Offering the Hand................· 126
Honoring Introductions................... 126
When Introductions are not Obligatory.................. 127
Always Introduce Guests.................................. 127
Additional Hints............ 128
STREET ETIQUETTE....................................... 131
Recognizing Friends........................ 133
Which Side of Pavement to Take.......................... 134
Stopping Acquaintances on Street........................ 134
Offering Assistance..................................... 135
The Use of Umbrellas................................. .. 135
Never Stop Lady on the Street............................ 135
Offering the Arm.. 135
How to Cross a Narrow Crossing.......................... 136
Ascending and Descending Stairs................ 136
Smoking in Presence of Ladies............................ 136
Shopping.. 137
Street Attire... 139
Form no Street Acquaintance............................ 139
Ladies alone at Night.................................... 139
Additional Notes.................................... 140
RIDING AND DRIVING...................................... 141
Gentle Mount.. 143
Punctuality... 144
Assisting Lady to Mount... 144
On the Road............. ....,....... 145
Assisting Lady to Dismount............. 145
The Seat of Honor....................................... 146
How to get in or out of Carriage......................... 146
Setting the Pace.. 147
Who shall Hold the reins..... 150
TRAVELING 151
Travel a great Civilizer.................................. 153
Ill Breeding shows Itself................................. 154

Being Polite.. 154
Offering and Accepting Courtesies 155
Gentlemen Smoking.. 155
Opening and Closing Windows 156
When a Lady may accept Courtesies................. 156
Lady with Escort................. 157
Tickets and Baggage.. 158
At the Hotel... 158
Additional Hints... 159
Sleeping Car........... 159
Securing and Occupying Seat................ 160
On Board Steamer............. 161
Being Sociable.. 161
Conversation 162
Traveling Abroad.. 162
Making Comparisons.. 162
PBLIC PLACES.. 165
Subdued, Reserved Manner.................................. 167
THE CHURCH............... 167
Reaching the Pew.............. 168
Use of Pews... 168
Conformity to mode of Worship............................. 169
Never go Late... 169
Additional Hints... 170
PLACES OF AMUSEMENT....................................... 170
Duty of Escort............... 171
Complete Quiet should be Maintained...................... 171
The Promenade between Acts................................. 172
Joining a Theatre Party.. 172
After-Theatre Calls............. 173
Inviting the Third Party....................................... 173
CHURCH FAIRS AND CHURCH BAZAARS.................. ... 173
Asking for Change.. 174
Deportment of Lady........... 174
UNDER THE GREENWOOD TREE............................... 175
Must be Plenty to Eat.. 175
Providing Conveyances... 176
The Popular Picnic.. 176
Ladies furnish the Dinner..................................... 177
Gentlemen make all Arrangements.......................... 177
After-Dinner Entertainment........... 178
Duty of Gentlemen to Entertain............................. 178

Great Latitude in Dress. 179
The Etiquette of Boating.................................... 179
Assisting Ladies to their Seats...... 179
Who Should Row... 180
A Popular Exercise....................................... 180
The Dress... 180
In the Gallery and Studio................................. 181
Invitations necessary..................................... 181
Proper Decorum in Studio................................. 181
Pricing Paintings... 182
Rude to Criticise Artist's Work........................... 183
Sitting for Portrait...................................... 183
Additional Hints.. 183
HOTELS.... 185
Ignorance betrays at once................................. 187
Advice to Gentlemen....................................... 188
Advice to Ladies.. 189
Arriving at Hotel... 189
Go and Come Quietly....................................... 189
Recognizing Friends....................................... 190
At Meals.. 190
In the Parlor... 191
Additional Hints.. 191
THE TABLE... 193
General Hints... 198
Begin to Eat as soon as Helped............................ 202
Knife, Fork and Spoon..................................... 202
Eating Asparagus.. 203
Eating Cherries, Plums, etc............................... 203
Finger Bowls.. 203
Conversation.. 203
DINNERS... 205
Dinner-Giving... 209
Number of Guests.. 210
Seating Guests.. 210
Conversation 211
Young Guests Spoil a Dinner Party......................... 212
Dishes not Placed on Table................................ 212
The Table... 212
The Dining-Room... 213
The Servants.. 213
Grace... 214

Prolonged Wine-drinking Condemned...................... 214
Length of Dinner.. 214
The Eye should have a Feast................................. 215
A Vexed Question... 215
Some Golden Rules... 216
Where Old Rules Prevail..................................... 217
Duties of Hostess... 218
Duties of Host.. 218
BALLS... 221
Wall-flowers.. 223
Assemble at 10 o'clock....................................... 223
Receiving Guests... 223
Gentleman Escorting Lady.................................... 224
Gentleman Unaccompanied by Lady........................... 224
Etiquette of Ball Room....................................... 224
Securing Partners.. 225
Supper at Midnight.. 227
Escorting Lady Home... 227
Additional Hints... 227
PRIVATE ENTERTAINMENT................................... 229
Receiving Guests... 231
Avoid Fussiness.. 232
Entertaining... 232
Hostess sees that Conversation does not Drag............... 232
Music and Dancing... 233
Ices... 233
Inviting Guests to Sing or Play.............................. 233
Preserving Order.. 234
Gentleman Escorts Lady to Piano............................ 234
Playing an Accompaniment................................... 235
PRIVATE THEATRICALS.. 235
Conversation.. 235
Making Comments on Instruments............................ 236
Turning Music... 236
Hostess makes Programme.................................... 236
The Hours for Private Theatricals........................... 237
Refreshments.. 237
Great Tact Required... 237
Much of your Pleasure depends upon Yourself............... 238
FUNERALS... 239
An Occasion of Sorrow....................................... 243
Avoid too Great Display..................................... 244

Funeral Director.. 245
Announcement.. 245
Order of Carriages... 245
Order at Funerals.. 246
Do not Arrive too Early................................... 246
Viewing the Remains...................................... 247
Order of Departure.. 247
At the Grave.. 247
Uncovering the Head...................................... 248
The Use of Flowers 248
Pall-bearers... 248
Gloves and Crape... 249
Visits of Condolence....................................... 249
Death of Members of a Society........................... 249
Additional Notes.. 250
MOURNING... 251
Period of Mourning....................................... 254
Seclusion from Society.................................... 255
Gentlemen in Mourning................................... 255
Children in Mourning..................................... 255
Additional Notes.. 256
CALLS AND VISITS... 257
Morning Calls... 259
Returning Visits.. 259
Visits of Ceremony.. 259
Never keep Visitor waiting................................ 260
Gentlemen's Morning Calls................................ 260
Pay Respects first to Hostess............................. 261
Introductions... 261
Departing... 261
Duties of Hostess... 262
Hints on Dress.. 262
Visits of Friendship....................................... 263
In England.. 263
Hospitality.. 264
Duties of Guest... 264
Entertaining Guest.. 266
Additional Hints.. 266
CONVERSATION.. 269
An Entertaining Talker the result of Study.............. 273
A Full Mind and Confidence............................... 274
The Art of Listening...................................... 275

Proper Subjects for Conversation........................... 276
Avoid Talking Shop... 277
Carefully avoid your " Hobby ".............................. 278
Wit that Wounds... 279
Do not Interrupt a Speaker................................. 279
Manner of Speaking... 279
Thinking Twice... 280
Keep your Temper.. 280
Do not Comment on infirmities of others.................... 280
The Abject Man... 281
Moderate your Expressions.................................. 281
Additional Hints... 282
LETTERS.. 285
The Modern Style... 287
Penmanship.. 288
Stationery... 289
Folding, Sealing and Stamping.............................. 290
A Questionable Improvement................................ 290
Use Black Ink.. 291
Writing Notes.. 291
How to begin a Letter...................................... 291
The Closing of a Letter.................................... 292
Neatness... 292
Underscoring... 292
Mourning Paper.. 293
Enclosing Stamps.. 293
Never Display Ill-temper in a Letter....................... 293
Every Letter should be Answered............................ 293
Never use Scraps of Paper.................................. 294
Additional Hints... 294
INVITATIONS.. 295
In whose Name to issue Invitations......................... 297
Answering Invitations...................................... 297
Keeping the Engagement.................................... 298
When Father entertains for Daughter, etc................... 298
Invitation to " At Homes".................................. 298
Forms of Invitations 299
Invitations Two Weeks in Advance.......................... 300
When Invitations must include Husband and Wife............ 300
How to send Invitations.................................... 300
Stationery... 301
Replying to Invitations.................................... 301

Invitations to Persons in Mourning.................. 302
Invitations to Members of Large Family.................. 302
Additional Notes.. 302
DRESS.. 305
The Bath.. 307
The Teeth... 308
The Hands... 308
The Hair.. 309
The Complexion.. 309
The Attire.. 310
Avoid Extremes.. 310
Selecting Materials................................... 310
Avoid trying Contrasts in Colors...................... 311
Neatness and Elegance................................. 311
The Low-necked Dress.................................. 312
Plain Satins and Velvets, etc......................... 312
Lacing.. 312
Study Harmony of Colors............................... 312
WASHINGTON ETIQUETTE 315
President and Family.................................. 317
Washington Society.................................... 317
Official Rank... 318
Official Calls.. 320
Reception Days.. 321
Etiquette of Receptions............................... 322
The White House....................................... 323
Social Etiquette under President Jefferson............ 324
STATIONERY... 327
Invitation to a Church Wedding........................ 329
Invitation to a Home Wedding.......................... 330
Announcement of Marriage.............................. 331
Formal Invitation to Dinner........................... 332
Informal Dinner Invitation............................ 333
An Informal Regret to Dinner.......................... 334
Formal Acceptance, Dinner Invitation.................. 335
An Invitation to Tea.................................. 336
Blank Card for Dinner Invitations..................... 336
Invitation to Theatre Party 337
Invitation to Breakfast............................... 337
Invitation to Small Dance............................. 338
Present Styles in Cards............................... 339

OUR MANNERS AND SOCIAL CUSTOMS.

ORIGIN OF CUSTOMS.

It is a curious and interesting fact that nearly all our social customs and ceremonials had their origin in militant times, and are referable to the practices of sanguinary savages. The polite bow of the modern Chesterfield is at best an elegant reminiscence of the servile prostration of some remote captive before his captor. Ceremonial forms have been naturally initiated by the relation of conqueror and conquered. From the whipped cur which, crawling on its belly, licks its master's hand, to the courtier who kneels before his king and kisses the royal fingers, may seem a long step, yet the connection between the two acts is clear. Both imply submission and their historic relation is almost obvious.

When the gentleman nods his head to a friend or an acquaintance he may not be aware of its primary significance. Yet it plainly refers to an act of submission on the part of an inferior to a superior. The savage captor cut off his captive's head. Sometimes he preferred to enslave his victim, and so spared him, merely requiring him to prostrate himself in the attitude of one about to be beheaded. Eventually this latter practice prevailed. The conquered were not slain, but held in bondage, the conqueror being propitiated by an offer of their heads, signified at first by a complete prostration and successively by kneeling and by profound inclinations of the body. The evolution to the present form of the ceremony is clearly traceable through many modifications and variations; and when you nod to a friend you signify that your head is his if he chooses to take it.

And when the hat is lifted something of a similar nature is implied. The conquered man, prostrate before his con- queror, and becoming himself a possession, simultaneously loses possession of whatever things he has about him; and therefore, surrendering his weapons, he also yields up, if the victor demands it, whatever part of his dress is worth taking. Hence the nakedness, partial or complete, of the captive, be- comes additional evidence of his subjugation. That it was so regarded of old in the East, there is clear proof. In Isaiah xx: 2–4, we read: "And the Lord said, like as my servant Isaiah hath walked naked and barefoot three years for a sign . . . so shall the king of Assyria lead away the Egyptians prisoners, and the Egyptians captives, young and old, naked and barefoot." The Assyrians completely stripped their captives; and in the Afghan war the Afreedees were reported to have stripped certain of their prisoners. Naturally, then, the taking off and yielding up of clothing becomes a mark of political submission, and in some cases even a com- plimentary observance, as in Fiji and Tahiti. In Samoa the complimentary act of unclothing is greatly abridged; only the girdle is removed.

With such facts before us, we can scarcely doubt that

surrender of clothing originates those obeisances which are made by uncovering the body more or less extensively. All degrees of uncovering have this meaning. The unhatting in England and America is equivalent to the uncloaking which is observed in Spain and the disrobing prevalent in less civilized communities; and all these are merely remnants of that process of unclothing himself by which, in early times, the captive expressed the yielding up of all he had.

The origin of handshaking is not less interesting. The inferior, as a token of subjection, offers to kiss a superior's hand. This offer is resisted by the superior, if he is condescending, and a conflict ensues, terminating in the inferior kissing his own hand to the superior. "Two Arabs of the desert, meeting," says Niebuhr, "shake hands more than ten times. Each kisses his own hand, and still repeats the question, 'How art thou?' . . . In Yemen, each does as if he wished the other's hand, and draws back his own to avoid receiving the same honor. At length to end the contest, the eldest of the two suffers the other to kiss his fingers." And here, according to Herbert Spencer, we find the origin of shaking hands. "If of two persons each wishes to make an obeisance to the other by kissing his hand, and each out of compliment refuses to have his own hand kissed, what will happen?" he inquires. "Just as when leaving a room, each of two persons, proposing to give the other precedence, will refuse to go first, and there will result at the doorway some conflict of movements, preventing either from advancing; so if each of two tries to kiss the other's hand, and refuses to have his own kissed, there will result a raising of the hand of each by the other toward his own lips, and by the other of a drawing of it down again, and so on alternately. Though at first such an action will be irregular," he continues, "yet as fast as the usage spreads, and the failure of either to kiss the other's hand becomes a recognized issue, the motions may be expected to grow regular and rhythmical. Clearly the difference between the simple squeeze, to which this salute is now often abridged, and the old-fashioned hearty shake, exceeds the differences between the hearty shake and the movement that would result from the effort of each to kiss the hand of the other."

But even in the absence of this clue yielded by the Arab custom, we should be obliged to infer some such genesis. No one can suppose, in view of all the facts, that hand-shaking was ever deliberately fixed upon as a complimentary observance, and if it had a natural origin in some act which, like bowing and unhatting, expressed subjection, the act of kissing the hand must be assumed as alone capable of leading to it.

The custom of exchanging presents, however, had its genesis in a natural desire to please. Travelers coming in contact with strange peoples, habitually propitiate them with gifts, by which two results are achieved. Gratification caused by the worth of the thing given tends to beget a friendly mood in the person approached; and there is a tacit expression of the donor's desire to please, which has a like effect.

But there is a very clear relation between mutilation and presents—between offering a part of the body and offering something else. The savage conqueror was propitiated by the conquered, first by yielding his entire person; then by yielding some portion of it, as a hand, a finger, or an ear; and finally by yielding some valuable possession, as his dress, his ornaments, or his weapons. Gradually the act of presentation passed into a ceremony expressing the wish to conciliate, things of no intrinsic value being sometimes substituted for things of real value. How natural is this substitution of a nominal giving for a real giving, where a real giving is impracticable, we are shown even by intelligent animals, as Herbert Spencer has observed. A retriever, accustomed to please his master by fetching killed birds, will fall into the habit at other times of fetching things to show his desire to please. On first seeing in the morning some one he is friendly with, he will add to his demonstrations of joy the seeking and bringing in his mouth a dead leaf, a twig, or any small available object lying near.

Yet natural as this propitiatory act of present-making is, it is worth noticing that among those peoples where militancy is not dominant, where the tribes are headless, or where the headship is feeble, the giving of gifts does not become an established usage. Along with the absence of strong personal rule among wild American and Australian races we find that there is a corresponding absence of gift-making as a political or social observance. In sharp contrast come accounts of the usages of the ancient Mexican and Peruvian civilizations. In these militancy was dominant; personal rule was strong; and no one went to salute his lord or king without a gift in his hand. In Tahiti, "whoever asks a favor of a chief, or seeks civil intercourse with him, is expected to bring a present." And here we see how making presents passes from a voluntary into a compulsory propitiation. The Tahitian chiefs, we are told, plundered the plantations of their subjects at will, the chiefs taking the property and persons of others by force. Hence it becomes manifest that present-making develops into the giving of a part to prevent loss of the whole. It is the policy at once to satisfy cupidity and to express submission.

The evidence from all sources implies that from propitiatory presents, voluntary and exceptional to begin with but becoming as political power strengthens less voluntary and more general, there eventually grow up universal and involuntary contributions—established tribute, and that with the rise of currency this passes into taxation. Similarly the gratuities of the king to his subject eventually lose their voluntary and exceptional character and become fixed perquisites or a settled salary. Judicial services in old times, even in England, were to be had only by giving the judge some valuable gift. These gifts were at first voluntary, but they finally became compulsory. And so with all other functionaries. At first supported by the voluntary presents of those who sought their favor, the gifts gradually become compulsory and ultimately settled into fixed fees and salaries. Before men received wages they were the recipients of largesse from kings and dukes and over-lords. Before the judge received a salary, he took bribes from both sides. And before th Ling received a revenue from taxes his state was supported by the voluntary offerings of those subjects who sought his immediate favor.

Even in its purely social aspect, the custom of present-making still retains something of its original character, although it is chiefly resorted to as an expression of good-will or of affection. However, we see in it here and there lingering traces of its militant associations. Subordinates seek to conciliate their superior by a costly gift, accompanied by a flattering speech; the employe courts the favor of the employ. er through the medium of a birthday or a wedding present; the political aspirant seeks to open the door of patronage by graceful complimentary testimonials to the administrative chief who holds the key.

It will sound strange to many that even the ceremony of visiting is of militant origin. It formerly signalized an act of submission, rendered by the subject to the sovereign. In countries where the social organization is feeble, where personal rule is weak, the ceremony of visiting is not common. Where power is centralized, it becomes imperative, and it becomes an expression of loyalty. As despotism declines and industrialism advances, the visit gradually loses its distinctive political character, and in the substitution of cards for calls, we may observe a growing tendency to dispense with it altogether as a formality of social intercourse.

Equally strange to most readers will appear the statement that the badges and costumes of civilized society are

directly traceable to savage habits and customs. The badge
is derived from the trophy, with which, in the early stage, it
is identical, and the dress, like the badge, is at first worn
not for warmth or propriety, but to excite admiration.   Indeed, it is inferable from certain known facts, that the costume is a collateral development of the badge, and the ornament has the same origin.

We might trace other modern usages to their source,
but the foregoing will perhaps suffice to show that our politest
acts and civilest ceremonies are linked with the rude and
bloody practices of a savage ancestry. Even the gallant who
removes his glove to touch the lily hand of his lady love re-
calls by the act the time when steel gauntlets were the prevailing fashion. And when he gives his right hand to his
friend, it is in proof of peace. The right hand is the sword
hand and its extension is a safe-guard against treachery.

So also in modern marriage ceremonials there are
reminiscences and survivals of barbaric practices. Among
primitive peoples the bride was carried off by force. She became the captive and by that fact the slave of her savage
admirer, whose love was fierce even if it were not tender. In
latter times, when civilization began to dawn, the bride was
not stolen ; her admirer bought her, sometimes with flocks or
herds, in other cases by the rendering of personal services,
as we read in Genesis xxix: 15-20: "And Laban said unto
Jacob, because thou art my brother, shouldst thou therefore
serve me for nought? tell me, what shall thy wages be?
And Laban had two daughters: the name of the elder was

Leah, and the name of the younger was Rachel. Leah was tender-eyed; but Rachel was beautiful and well formed. And Jacob loved Rachel and said, I will serve thee seven years for Rachel, thy youngest daughter, and Laban said, It is better that I give her to thee, than that I should give her to another man; abide with me. And Jacob served seven years for Rachel, and they seemed unto him but a few days, for the love he had to her." The wild Indian of America to this day exchanges ponies for a bride; and there are not wanting instances of purchase and sale even in much higher circles, where American daughters are bartered to titled European profligates and to blasé millionaires for family advantage.

That the savage tradition still lingers in the modern etiquette of marriage is variously shown. We even yet say that a man "carries away his bride," and we treat the lover up till the last vow has been exchanged and the last forms complied with as a sort of amicable foe and the object of his devotion as a precious trust to be sacredly guarded from him who seeks to bear her off. Thus this theory survives in England where only the carriage which bears the newly wed away on their honeymoon is furnished by the groom. The other carriages are furnished by the father of the bride, who acknowledges no proprietorship in his daughters but his own until the last act of the ceremony has been concluded. In America, in some instances, even this much is not permitted to the groom, the father of the bride furnishing the carriage that conveys the bride and groom on the first stage of their wedding journey. The groom furnishes nothing but the

ring and the bride's bouquet, with presents for the bridesmaids and his best man, and some appropriate favor for the
ushers.   He also buys the license and fees the minister.

But it is not of ancient customs and usages that we design to treat, but of their outgrowth in modern manners.
And who, says Emerson, does not delight in fine manners?
Their charm, he adds, cannot be predicted or over-stated.
"Manners," said Edmund Burke, the great English states-
men, "are of more importance than laws.   Upon those in a
great measure the law depends.   The law teaches us but
here and there, now and then.   Manners are what vex and
sooth, comfort or purify, exalt or debase, barbarize or refine
us, by a constant, steady, uniform, insensible operation, like
that of the air we breathe in.   They give their whole form
and color to our lives.   According to their quality, they aid
morals, they supply laws, or they totally destroy them."

While we have seen that most of our social usages had
their genesis in militancy and were developed under slavery
and fear, we must not forget to note the happy transition
which has brought us to do from generous impulse and
kindly instinct what our remote ancestry did from baseness
or compulsion.   No doubtful motive discredits the politeness
that distinguishes refined society. We are not obliging through
fear or sycophancy.   Our cordial hand-shake is a token of
amity without submission.   It expresses both fellowship and
equality.   We assist the fallen, protect the weak and reverence the aged, not in the hope of reward or for personal
vain-glory, but in obedience to that New Commandment
"That ye love one another."

And, indeed, a perfect society would be one in which this sweetest commandment were the rule of life. We can not conceive of really bad manners among people who obey this divine injunction. Yet people who actually love one another, from inadvertence or want of reflection, may sometimes appear inconsiderate and even rude, so that the best disposed and kindliest hearts need discipline—and where shall they get it unless at home?

The home influence in the formation of manners is all-important. As the twig is bent the tree's inclined, and as the boy and girl are trained at home, so will they continue in after life. It is hard to make a silk purse out of a sow's ear, say the Spanish, and so it is not easy even by the gentlest influences of parents and home to refine a coarse nature. Yet even the rudest boy and the most hoydenish girl are not beyond improvement, if properly handled. The obligation rests on every parent to make the most and the best of his children in this respect, for their position in life will largely depend upon the manner in which they have been fitted for the discharge of its duties and the enjoyment of its social amenities.

In the chapters which follow we shall endeavor to enforce this obligation upon fathers and mothers, while pointing out the relief that govern good society, and at the same time the duty of children will be made clear and in like manner pressed home upon them. It will rest with the reader whether there is profit for him in the precepts and examples here brought together into serviceable form.

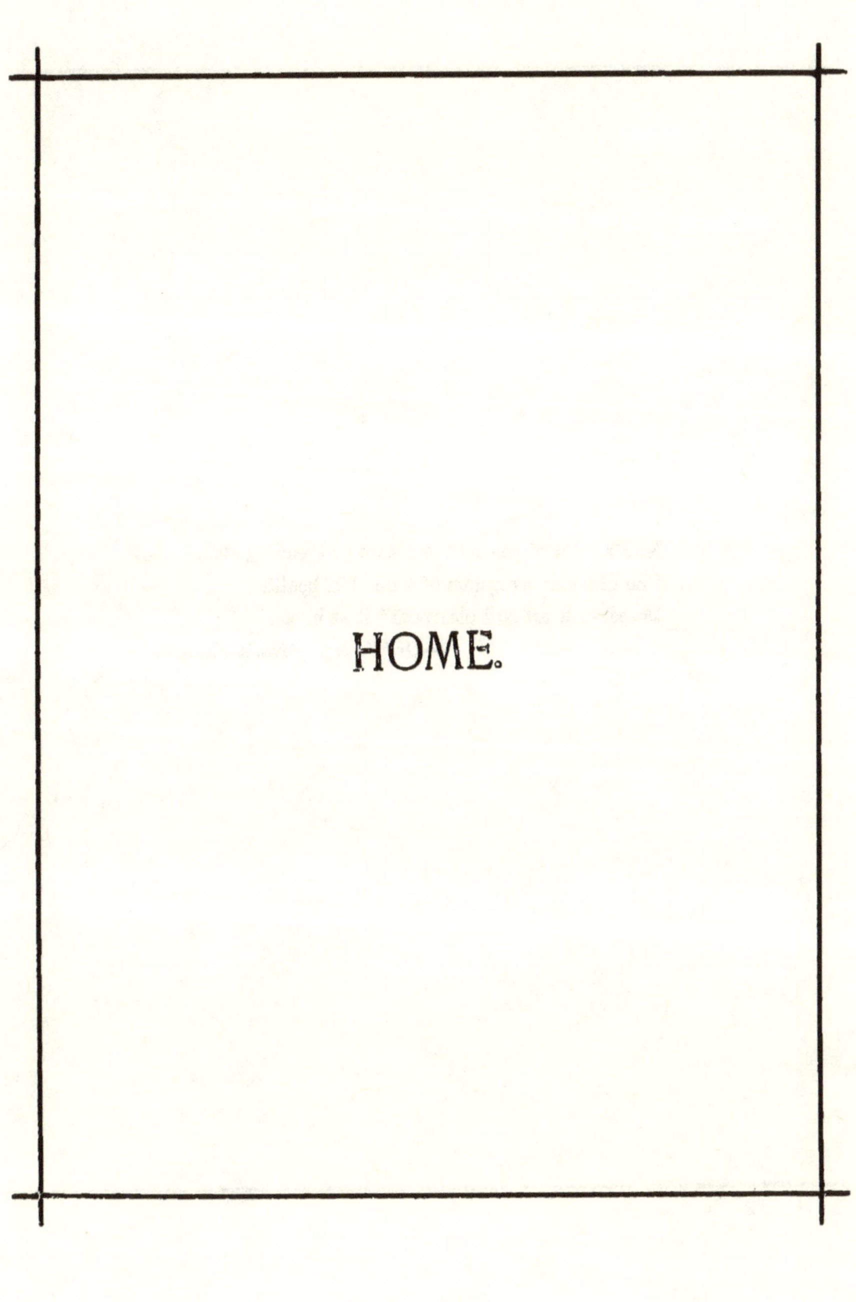

HOME.

Man's greatest strength is shown in standing still:
The first sure symptom of a mind in health
Is rest of heart and pleasures felt at home.
                          —Dᴿ. *Young: "Night Thoughts."*

HOME.

Home! There is no word in the English language so full of meaning. There is no word that so thrills the wanderer and none that carries to his mind a tenderer significance and a purer joy. Nor is it to the wanderer alone that it brings its freightage of bright memories and sweet suggestions. To the tired clerk behind the counter, to the grave judge upon the bench, to the plodding plowman in the furrow, to the statesman in the halls of legislation, it comes to cheer, to strengthen and to bless.

But the picture were not complete without its shadings and backgrounds. It is not to every one that home is a shrine. While to many it may mean wife and children and light and music, to others it may suggest far different scenes and accessories. To one, home means love at the hearth, a loaded table, a mansion filled with pictures and the treasures of art. To another, it may mean want, "looking out of a cheerless fire-grate, kneading hunger in an empty bread tray, the damp air shivering with curses." To one, home is the center of hope, the object of devotion, the inspiration of endeavor. It is not merely an abiding-place; it is a kingdom where Love sways the scepter with gentle and benignant authority. To another it is the resort of misery, the breeding place of vice, the nursery of crime. There is no Bible or good books on the shelf. The children are old before their time, corrupted with evil and infected with disease. In the background stands want, while sin stares from the front. No Sabbath wave ever rolls over the door sill. That home is a furnace for forging everlasting chains, and gathering faggots for an unending funeral pile. It is spelled with curses, it weeps with ruin, it chokes with woe, it sweats with the death agony of despair.

But it is of the true home that we here desire to speak. It is the hearth around which cluster domestic joys that commands our thought. It is to a region of sunshine and hope that we invite your presence.

To Adam, says Hare, Paradise was a home; to the good among his descendants home is a paradise. And it is at the family fireside where a man's real self is disclosed. There he throws off the little disguises in which he appears before the world and we behold him in his true character. John Howard, the philanthropist, as the world saw him, was a man of wide and beneficent sympathies. He succeeded in mitigating the horrors of prison life and his influence for good extended beyond his own country and his own time. Yet John Howard was a tyrant in his own home, and by neglect he suffered his son to fall into dissolute habits which ended in madness. On the other hand we see Burns "convulsed by volcanic passion" a model of domestic devotion; and Luther, "as wild as the storm that uproots the oak" in public, is at home "as gentle as the zephyr that dallies with the violet."

Napoleon was tempestuous and tyrannical in camp and court, yet more than one astonished courtier saw him upon

The Home.

⊿is hands and knees in the nursery to which he often escaped from the cabinet.

The Sage of Chelsea was called barbarous in his rudeness before the world, yet to his wife he was the soul of tenderness and chivalric devotion. But illustrations need not be multiplied. These suffice to show that men often go about in disguises which they lay aside when at home. Before the public they pose and attitudinize. In the light of their own firesides they stand forth as nature made them.

Yet not every man puts on a mask when he steps across his threshold. Longfellow's books and public acts reflect a faithful picture of his private life. Audubon was blessed with an even temper which rendered him superior to accidents that to another might have brought despair. Having spent years in the forest with gun and pencil, bringing down and sketching the beautiful birds, till his manuscript was complete, he paused for a rest of a few days before having his work printed. He left the precious manuscript in a trunk at Philadelphia, but in his absence, rats utterly destroyed the results of his years of toil. He did not rave nor tear his hair. He was a little disappointed, but without the least exhibition of temper, he picked up his gun and pencil and again visited the great forests of America. Such a man is worth a study. Such a life as his is worthy of imitation. He was always unassuming and he never spoke of his own life but with gratitude to heaven that so much of happiness had been his portion. A great worker, to him home was a place of rest, of pleasure, of recreation;—it was the source of inspiration and a refuge from the great turbulent world around.

Consider home as a refuge, and how vigilantly and tenderly it should be guarded! How carefully should sentinels of love and duty hedge it about! "Life," says Talmage, "is the United States army on the national road to Mexico, a long march, with ever and anon a skirmish and a battle. At eventide we pitch our tent and stack the arms, we hang up the war-cap and lay our heads on the knapsack, and we sleep until the morning bugle calls us to marching and action. How pleasant it is to rehearse the victories and the surprises and the attacks of the day, seated by the still camp fires of the home circle!

"Yea, life is a stormy sea. With shivered masts and torn sails, and bulk aleak, we put in at the harbor of home. Blessed harbor! There we go for repairs in the dry dock of quiet life. The candle in the window is to the toiling man the lighthouse guiding him into port. Children go forth to meet their fathers as pilots of the Narrows take the hand of ships. The door-sill of the home is the wharf where heavy life is unladen."

But home is something more than a refuge. It is a citadel of the state. Break up the home and you destroy the nation. The state is held together by moral principle, and that kind of principle is the outgrowth of family relations. No home means a wandering life, a wandering life means barbarism, and barbarism means unstable government. The virtues that cement the home are the strength and the glory of the nation, the safeguard of political institutions.

INFLUENCE OF HOME.

Moreover, home is a school where all virtues are taught and practiced. It is the university whence come all the noble men and women who adorn the varied walks of life. From its sacred precincts every thing that degrades should be shut out. All that elevates should be cultivated. "As the Roman sentinel stands in front of the city, the sunlight casts his shadow upon the wall, and the impression thus made will remain till the elements have dissolved the solid rock." And so the lessons of this home school will sink deep into the receptive mind of the child. Early impressions will survive the mutations of time. Every word or act, every burst of temper or harsh look, every gentle glance or amiable deed will leave its indelible impress upon the young. How important then it is that the curriculum of the home should be prudently and prayerfully chosen! How vital it is that every lesson should reflect the good, the true and the beautiful!

GREAT RESPONSIBILITY.

A fearful responsibility thus rests upon the teachers in the home school. It is with them to make or to mar the minds entrusted to their charge. They train either to honor or to disgrace, to fame or to failure, to heaven or to perdition. The responsibility cannot be escaped. The home and the street are the formative influences surrounding the child. If the attractions of home, if its sympathies and services, are wanting, then the street claims its prey. The child becomes at once the pupil and the victim of the highway, innocence learns the tricks of vice, and a sweet vessel is filled with slime and corruption.

MAKE HOME ATTRACTIVE.

The home school must be bright. Its attractions should out shine those of the outer world. Pictures, music, innocent gayeties should charm the wayward fancy of childhood and keep it from straying. A dark home makes bad boys and bad girls in preparation for bad men and bad women. It is therefore our duty to take into our home circles all innocent hilarity, all brightness and all good cheer.

"The little community to which I gave laws," said the Vicar of Wakefield, "was regulated in the following manner: We all assembled early, and after we had saluted each other with proper ceremony (for I always thought fit to keep up some mechanical forms of good breeding, without which freedom ever destroys friendship,) we all knelt in gratitude to that Being who gave us another day. So also when we parted for the night."

Here we have a noble precept and a worthy example. The courtesies of society, even in trivial matters, should never be omitted; and the head of that house in which the voice of thanksgiving is not heard may not reasonably expect the blessings of heaven.

DUTIES OF A WIFE.

But it is upon the wife that the happiness of home chiefly depends. It is her privilege and pleasure to promote domestic felicity and garland her husband's house with the flowers of a sweet and helpful life. It is to her, therefore, that we would first address ourselves, and we would most earnestly urge her at the very outset, as she enters beneath her husband's roof as a bride, to avoid giving the man of her choice any cause for complaint in those little details of personal habit and conduct where she is so likely to fail. As a sweetheart she has studied to please. As a wife should she do less? Nay, should she not do more? Has not her vow made what was a privilege an imperative duty?

OWES FIRST DUTY TO HOME.

The young wife will find many temptations awaiting her. There will be excellent people, with zeal beyond their discretion, who will assail her with propositions which she should not too hastily accept. She will be wanted to devote a portion of her time to this charity or that. She will be urged to become a school or district visitor, or there will be sewing circles and fairs for which her support will be solicited. These are all laudable in themselves, but the young wife will not suffer them to engage her thought and leisure without the husband's full concurrence. Nor will she go to evening lectures except in his company. It were a fatal mistake to leave him to spend his evenings alone.

STRIVE TO PLEASE.

She should wear her good manners at home as well as abroad. She can not afford to appear more agreeable in company than when she sits at her own fireside. Marriage more than once has proven a failure simply because the wife has neglected in the domestic circle the arts of her sex which render her an object of admiration in society. Nothing can be more fatuous than the conduct of a young woman whc seeks to be admired by the world for her taste and engaging manners, or for her skill in music, yet makes no effort to render her home attractive. But still that home, whether a mansion or a flat, is the very center for her life—the nucleus around which her affections should gather, and beyond which she has small concerns.

AVOID CONFIDANTS.

The confidant is to be studiously avoided. The young wife will be on her guard against entrusting any individual whatever with the secrets of her domestic annoyances. There are those who are ever ready to gain a dangerous ascendancy in families by courting the confidence of young wives. Shun these as you would a pestilence; and should any one presume to offer you advice with regard to your husband, or seek to lessen him in your estimation by insinuations, avoid that person as you would a serpent. Many a happy home has been made desolate by exciting suspicion, or by endeavors to gain importance in an artful and insidious manner.

PRACTICE ECONOMY.

The young wife can not be too careful in her expenditures. She should act openly and honorably in all questions of money, keeping her accounts with scrupulous accuracy and studying her husband's interests in every detail of household economy. "My husband works hard for every dollar he earns," said the young wife of a professional man, as she sat sewing a button on her husband's coat, "and it seems to me worse than cruel to lay out a dime unnecessarily." This was in the right spirit and she must indeed have been a helpmeet to the man whose name she bore. No more should be spent by the wife for dress than her husband's income will justify and the same economy should prevail in furnishing her parlors and bedrooms. There should be no concealment in regard to money concerns. No important purchase should ever be made by the wife without the knowledge and consent of her husband.

HOME ADORNMENTS.

No effort should be spared in adorning the home **and** the sitting-room above all should be bright and cheerful. Natural ornaments and flowers tastefully arranged give an air of elegance to a room in which the furniture is far from costly; and books judiciously placed uniformly produce a good effect. The power of association is very great and no sensible wife will underestimate the influence on her husband of comfortable and tasteful domestic surroundings.

AVOID BICKERING.

Nor will she less painstakingly avoid all bickerings. What does it signify where a picture hangs, or whether a rose or a pink shall be set to adorn the parlor table? A small concession will often prevent a serious misunderstanding; the graceful yielding of a favorite opinion, where neither honor nor principle is involved, will promote good feeling and disarm the hastiest temper. In the woman who is married to a man disposed to irascibility the wisest discretion is demanded. If she fail to command her own temper, that of her husband is certain to be tried and bitter heart-burnings will follow. She will seek by every possible means to prevent him from committing himself in her presence and she will find the reward of her self-control in an ultimate mastery of his passions. She will lead him whither he could not have been driven.

COMMANDING RESPECT.

The woman who forgets that she is a lady must not expect her husband to remember it. If she approve a mean action, if she fail in refinement, if she grow careless of her conduct, with what reason may she expect to command the husband's respect and confidence? If she lack reverence for her self and her exalted position as wife and mother, why should she hope to hold the reverential regard of the man who sees her moral declension? The slightest duplicity destroys confidence. The least want of refinement in conversation, or in the selection of books, lowers a woman, aye, and forever!

These few precepts apply to every class of society; and to the woman who shall duly observe them may be accorded the beautiful commendation of Solomon when recording the words which the mother of King Lemuel taught him: "The heart of her husband doth safely trust in her; she will do him good, and not evil, all the days of her life. Strength and honor are her clothing: and she shall rejoice in time to come. Her children rise up and call her blessed; her husband also, and he praiseth her."—Prov. xxxi.

Inviting Grounds.

DUTIES OF THE HUSBAND.

But if the wife have her duties, so has the husband his. The burden, or, rather the privilege, of making home happy is not the wife's alone. There is something demanded of the lord and master and if he fail in his part, domestic misery must follow, let the wife strive for happiness as she will. The husband should not forget that his obligation is great. He has won a gentle and confiding creature and removed her from all she had previously held most dear in association and companionship; he has sworn to love and to cherish, as she has sworn to honor and obey; and it is his high privilege and sweet duty to make the new associations and companionship all that her fond fancy has pictured them. He should remember when he brings his bride home that he now has committed to his charge the happiness of another. Not his own convenience and pleasure alone, but the wife's, must be consulted, kindness and delicate attention are her due, and words and acts must be considered with chivalric regard for her gentle feelings and sensibitities.

SELF-CONTROL.

When small disputes arise, the husband will forbear. The wife's good sense must be given a chance to assert itself; and it is the man's prerogative to be strong. The husband who fails to master his own temper cannot hope to master that of his wife. We must study her happiness without yielding to her caprices and in the end he will have no reason to regret his self-control.

ACCOMPANY THE WIFE TO CHURCH.

The considerate husband will never let his wife go to church alone on Sunday. It is not a pleasant sight to see a young wife going toward the church-door unattended, alone in the midst of a crowd, with her thoughts dwelling, it may be sadly, on the time when her husband was proud to walk beside her. He ought to remember that the condition of the young bride is often a very solitary one, and that for his sake she has left her father's roof and the companionship of kindred and friends. Her days are spent without the light of any smile but her husband's and to deny her the courtesy of his company when she goes to the house of prayer is surely as ungenerous in him as it is unkind. In fact, it is a breach of domestic etiquette on the husband's part to stay at home while the wife goes forth alone to church. Sunday is the day of rest, wisely and mercifully appointed to loose the bonds by which men are held to the sordidness of the world; and the husband should spend it as becomes the head of a family. Let no temptation induce him to wish his wife to relinquish attendance upon divine services, merely that she may idle at home to beguile his hours. Religion is her safeguard and woe may be to the husband if he withdraw her from its protection!

MAKE A CONFIDENT OF THE WIFE.

Want of candor often brings its own punishment. Husbands conceal their affairs, yet expect their wives to act with economy and discretion. Is it any wonder that they sometimes meet disappointment? The plain duty of the husband is to make a frank statement of his income to his wife.   Otherwise she cannot properly regulate her expenses and he will be constantly in fear lest she pass the limit of his ability to pay.   Husband and wife ought to consult as to the sum that can be afforded for housekeeping and when this is arranged, he will find it advantageous to give into her hands, at stated intervals, the money required.

DO NOT INTERFERE WITH HOUSEHOLD MANAGEMENT.

The less he interferes with her management of the household the better it will be.   The home department belongs to the wife exclusively; the husband's province is to rule the house—her's to regulate its internal economy.   It is true that some young wives know little of household concerns. They may buy foolishly and waste much by reason of their inexperience.   But they should be dealt with patiently and in good temper.   A little advice, kindly and firmly given, will soon put them in the right way and keep them there.   And when the husband observes in his helpmeet a disposition to do right, let him not withhold a word of approbation.

WORDS OF ENCOURAGEMENT.

Let him be pleased with trifles and commend efforts to excel on every fitting occasion.   If the wife be diffident, let her be encouraged.   If she make mistakes, do not appear to see them.   It is unreasonable to add to the embarrassment of her new condition by ridiculing her deficiencies.   And do not indulge in invidious comparisons.   Your mother and sisters were undoubtedly superior in household arts, but forbear to

mention the fact.   Many a wife has been alienated from her
husband's family by injudicious and ungenerous references to
"the way mother did it" and the man who thus wounds a tender and susceptible heart is unworthy of its devotion.

BE AMIABLE AND AGREEABLE.

In conclusion, we urge every young married man who
wishes to render his home happy, to consider his wife as the
light of his domestic circle, and to permit no cloud, however
small, to darken the region in which she reigns. Most women
are naturally amiable, gentle and compliant; and if a wife
becomes perverse and indifferent to her home it is generally
her husband's fault. He should consult her happiness in
small things as in great. If she dislikes cigars—and few
young women want their clothes tainted by tobacco—leave
off smoking; for at best it is not a desirable habit. Read to
her, if she desires to hear you. Do not put your feet on a
chair and go to sleep. If she loves music, take her to the
concert as you were wont to do when you sought her for a
bride. The husband may say that he is tired. But was he
never tired in the courting days? He may declare he does
not like music. But did he never discover this till
he was safely married? Let him practice somewhat of self-
denial and let him reflect that no one acts with a due regard
for his own happiness who lays aside, when the honeymoon
is over, all those gratifying attentions which he was ever
alert to pay the lady of his love. He injures himself when
he neglects those rational sources of home enjoyment which

made her look forward with a bounding heart to become his companion through life.

Etiquette is a broad and comprehensive term and its observance nowhere more desirable than in the domestic circle.

BOYS.

Ah! happy years! once more who would not be a boy?
　　　　　　　　　　　　　—*Byron.*

·A boy's will is the wind's will,
And the thoughts of youth are long, long thoughts.
　　　　　　　　　　　　　--*Bryant.*

BOYS.

The boy is a perplexing study. It is more difficult to acquire a thorough knowledge of him than it is to master Greek and Latin and the higher mathematics. Each boy is a new text-book by a different author; and there is just enough variation in the matter and method to confuse the student. Some one has said of Shakespeare that he "has no style, because he has so many styles,—because he is forever coining new forms of expression, and breaking the mould as fast as they are coined." And so with boys. They have no style because they have so many styles. Selecting a model boy, you try to make your boy like the model, but you fail. You take Washington with his little hatchet, but your boy proves saving of his veracity. Or possibly Daniel Webster is chosen, but your boy turns out to be slow of speech and dull of apprehension. Perchance, like Sir Isaac Newton's parents, you decide that your boy is little higher in the intellectual scale than an idiot, but eventually he belies his early promise and astounds the world with his lofty genius.

CLASSIFYING BOYS.

Verily, boyhood is a study, but it is one of those studies not yet reduced to a science. Indeed, it is doubtful if we can ever reduce the study of boys to a science. It must always remain experimental. If we could frame a system of phi-

losophy on the subject, we should call it "Boyology"; but
when we come to a general classification of facts relating to
the boy, we find ourselves at fault. He refuses to be classi-
fied. If we start with the classifiction of "good and bad,"
we find that under the test of life it fails. Half the boys in
the "good" class turn out bad and many of those in the "bad"
class grow up good. So that classification will not do; and
if we start with "smart and dull," we come out no better, for
the smart boys, expending all their vitality in youth, grow up
to be dull, while Sheridan, Scott, Dickens, Goldsmith, Burns,
the dullest of their classes at school and the least promising
of their fellows in youth, became the master thinkers of their
day and the brightest lights of a luminous host. There is the
appearance of a classification in the wildness or tameness
of boyhood; and perhaps that will serve as a starting-point.
All boys are either wild or tame—they have either a tempest
or a calm locked within their breasts. If we cannot set our
stake here and say we have something settled and definite,
then truly boys are a hopeless enigma, and we may as well
confess first as last that we cannot understand them. All the
help the dictionary gives us on the subject is contained in the
statement that "a boy is a male child." But this really throws
no light upon it; we are left just as much in the dark as before. There is a common saying that "the child is father to
the man;" but this is no more enlightening, except as it
may show us that we owe a proper respect to our ancestry.

THE WILD BOY.

But to get back to our starting point—wild boys and tame. The tame boy is a sweet child, but he is not the sort of stuff that reformers and scholars and captains of industry are made of. The wild boy causes you more trouble while he is a child; but, if you have done your duty by him, he is the one that you regard with greatest pride when he is grown up, for he is alert, strong, masterful, full of ambition and achievement, a leader among men. Grass does not grow in his path; you do not have to find him something to do; he sees the opportunities of life for himself and takes them.

We often hear boys described as "good" or "bad." But there are no bad boys, unless we have transmitted evil qualities to them. To tell a boy that he is bad, either lowers you in his estimation, or it lowers himself. He either believes what you say, or he doubts it. If he believes you, he at once makes up his mind that it's no use trying. "I'm bad any way," he reflects, "I can't amount to anything, and I wont try." If he doesn't believe you, he will think, "Now, I can't depend on what my parents say. They say I'm bad, but I know that my intentions are good, and I should be judged by my intentions. Whatever they say hereafter, I'll accept with a good deal of allowance." We must not forget that the boy knows much more than we give him credit for. He usually understands his own motives, and if we call him bad when he knows that his motives were good, we wound him and lose his confidence. No parent can afford to stand low in his child's opinion. If he is bad, he is the last one who should know it.   Do all in your power to make him think he is not bad.   And after all, the bad boy is usually a boy wild with passion, like a spirited horse, and the important question is, "Who is going to hold the reins and do the driving? " If the boy's judgment and intellect hold them, then he will make the journey of life grandly, and with power that difficulties cannot subdue.   He will battle evil as a reformer.   He will conquer success in war or in traffic.   Every door in life will stand open to receive him, and he will run his course like a giant.   But if his passions are to hold the reins, then stand out of his way.   If he is bad, he is bad all over.   He is bad with just as much power as he would, in the other case, have been good.   Human life is nothing to him and his will is the wind's will, stirred to a tempest by every heat of passion.

Much depends on the way the boy is handled. If you help him to get control of himself, there is no danger; but if you manage him so as to leave the reins in the grasp of his passions, it is all danger.

The tame boy sits under the shade tree before the cottage door, like some delicate house plant that has been set out in the yard.   He is good to look at, but not worth much to use.   At the same time the war-whoop is heard upon the hillside or in the adjoining fields or woods.   That is the wild boy.   The hills and rocks mock him and send back his shout.   He accepts their challenge as he advances to vanquish his new-found enemy—the hills ring with shouts. He reaches the rocks above, but the voices that mocked him are gone, and again his victorious shout is heard.   He be.

comes acquainted with birds and flowers. The trees tell him their secrets. The habits and instincts of the smaller animals are his constant study. At night his cheeks bear the hues of the morning. Deal gently with him, O parents, for untold possibilities are there. He is wild with animal spirits. Do not try to drive him, but lead him gently, carefully. Gradually turn the current of his life in the direction of the work to be accomplished. Do not dam the stream, but keep it flowing and guide it as best you may. It may be said of boys that

> "Their lives are songs; God writes the words,
> And we set them to music at pleasure.
> And the song grows glad, or sweet or sad
> As we choose to fashion the measure.
> We must write the music whatever the song,
> Whatever its rhym or metre,
> And if it is glad we may make it sad,
> Or, if sweet, we may make it sweeter."

THE TAME BOY.

The tame boy is a negative element. He makes a good picture, and looks well when framed and hung up on the wall. But if he carries his tameness into manhood the world disdains him. If the world doesn't like a man, it says; "He is a very good or tame man." There is an undertone of irony in those words. The successful man will resent such a statement as an insult. Martin Luther was not one of your tame boys. He was endued with strong passions. If error presented itself he had the courage to attack it. A hurricane in youth, an avalanche in manhood, he became one of earth's greatest reformers. The wild boy is at a premium every time. He is gold or silver coin of full value. If you mutilate him, however, he depreciates. The tame boy is a greenback or bank note. You may mutilate him and he is worth no less than before. Tear off a corner and it makes no difference about his value. He never grows brighter by friction, but, on the contrary, grows dimmer till you can't use him any longer, because you can't tell what he is. He is not worth anything until a value is stamped on him, or coin has been deposited with which to redeem him. He is not worth anything out of his own country. The wild boy, if you have not clipped him by bad management, will pass in any country. You do not need to stamp a value upon him. That he always does for himself. He grows brighter by use and when he is nearly worn out, so you can't find the figures expressing his value, weigh him and keep him in circulation. A parent cannot afford to have tame children unless he is rich; neither can he afford to have wild children unless he has the patience and prudence to guide them.

THE STUDIOUS BOY.

But we must here distinguish studiousness from mere tameness. Some boys inherit an applied tendency. A nervous temperament is usually theirs, and unless carefully handled they will expend all their forces in childhood. If their strength can be husbanded so they enter manhood with vital forces unimpaired, they make profound scholars, inventors, great historians, philosophers and artists. They adorn any department of life in which their powers may find direction.

And as we must distinguish the studious boy from the merely tame boy, so must we observe the difference between the wild boy and the boy who has inherited the instincts of outlawry.

THE CRUEL BOY.

Cruelty seems to be instinctive in some boys. They have inherited that applied tendency. Benedict Arnold was constantly, and from cruel motives, torturing young birds and animals, and that disposition made him the execrated Arnold the traitor. The same tendency is in seen in Nero, the cruel emperor of Rome, who murdered his mother and his wife, who. burnt the imperial city and fiddled while the flames devoured its temples and palaces, and who died at last by his own hand. It is the same uncontrolled tendency that manifests itself in great criminals. Yet without doubt it can be controlled if taken in time.

THE EYE THE WINDOW OF THE SOUL.

"But," says the anxious parent, "how shall I know whether my boy is studious or tame, vicious or wild?" We answer: "The eye is the window of the soul." Men are like Geneva watches with crystal faces that expose the whole movement. The face and eyes reveal what the spirit is doing, how old it is, and what aims it has. An eye can threaten like a loaded and levelled gun, or, by means of kindness, can make the heart dance with joy. Eyes speak all languages. The communication by the glance is in the greatest part not subject

to the control of the will.   It is the bodily symbol of the iden-
tity of nature.   We look into the eyes to know if this other
form is another self, and the eyes will not lie, but makes faithful confession what inhabitation is there.   When the eye says
one thing and the tongue another, the practiced man relies on
the language of the eye.   If the man is off his center, the eyes
show it.   There are asking eyes, assenting eyes, prowling eyes,
and eyes full of fate—some of good and some of sinister omen.
Each man carries in his eye the exact indication of his rank
in the immense scale of men, and we are always learning to
read it.

The tame eye may be sleepy, or vacant, or it may show
depth of mere goodness.   The studious eye shows a deep,
steady and confident look.   It never drops, but meets your
level glance unflinchingly.   The cruel eye has a wild un-
steady glare—a fierce piercing look.   It drops before the
steady gaze of an honest eye.   The wild boy has a clear
sparkling eye.   Like the studious eye, it is concious of no
evil intent, and therefore it looks right into your eyes without
shrinking.   The wild or studious eye may drop from modesty
but the face reveals the cause.   But the cruel eye drops with
a sullen expression.   There are other methods of studying
the boy, but the eye is the true index to his character and
quality.

BE A TRUE PARENT TO THE BOY.

Then make a careful study of your boy. God grant that he
may grow up to be a comfort to your age and an honor to
society.   He makes you some trouble now, but he will not

bother long.   Nothing in the world grows as fast as children.
It seems only last week since your boy was playing with little toys, but now he is a man with a home of his own.   Then
his playthings were scattered all over the floor.   You were
neat and orderly; and it annoyed you to see the confusion
he caused in the appearance of your room.   Now it is orderly
enough.   It is too orderly and quiet!   Yes, it is quiet and orderly now.   There are no disputes to settle, no questions to
answer, no bruised fingers to tie up, no little clothes to be
mended, no sleepy boys to put to bed, no one to get ready
for school next day.   Dear parents, why are you so sad?
Why do the furrows deepen and the eyes grow dim and the
heart sad?   You wanted the house orderly, and it is so now.
You wanted it quiet, and is it not still?   You were annoyed
with the care of the boy, and are you not now relieved from
such burdens?   Wipe the tears from your eyes and be cheerful.   Why not be happy and joyous?   Ah, memory is too
faithful and hearts are too true!   It seemed as if the boy
would always be with you, but he has gone.   You did not
know how large a space in your hearts he filled until he grew
up and left you.   You long for one sound of his boyish voice,
and now the clatter of his feet upon the stairs would be music
to your ear.   With what fondness could you now kiss his
eyes to sleep!   O! how willingly could you now answer all his
questions and how tenderly lead him in the way of truth and
usefulness!

BOYS MUST BATTLE IN LIFE.

But the boy must grow and he must face the great future which looms with possibilities and beckons with bright hopes. He must prepare himself for the outset and struggle. Giants will come out to meet him on the way and these must be disarmed. Difficulties will arise which he alone may overcome. Obstacles will resist his progress which he, and not another for him, must surmount. He must be equipped for a desperate hand-to-hand contest with stubborn foes that will dispute every inch of his forward path. Either he must bravely fight or weakly perish. He cannot go through life unchallenged. Strong soul and high endeavor, he will need them both. "Lo! here, now, in our civilized society, the old allegories yet have a meaning, the old myths are still true. Into the valley of the shadow of Death yet often leads the path of duty, through the streets of Vanity Fair walk Christian and Faithful, and on Great-heart's armor ring the clanging blows. Ormuzd still fights with Ahriman—the Prince of Light with the Powers of Darkness. He who will hear, to him the clarions of the battle call."

"Of the myriads of human beings who flit across the stage of life, but few, comparatively," says an eloquent biographer of the late George Peabody, "ever become really eminent; but few ever thrust themselves, so to speak, unwittingly, it may be, upon the popular observation, or organize and achieve a marked success. But few are willing to burst the shackles of sensuous thraldom, and gird on the whole panoply of a true and elevated manhood, and enter the arena of life's conflict, yielding to the nobler impulses of the higher nature, the intellectual and moral, necessitating the complete subserviency of the lower and mere animal nature. But few raise high the standard of attainment, basing the purposes of life upon clear and vivid ideas and potent aspirations, and then concentrate the developed and expanding energies of the soul with pertinacious and indomitable courage. These few stand out in bold relief like the majestic oak on the hill-top, or like some bright particular star, suddenly emerging from the horizon, moving upward in majesty, full-orbed and radiant, increasing in size and brilliancy, and sending its beams of light to the remotest regions. Some of these remind us of the meteor as it dashes across the heavens, blazing with its own native fires; sometimes seemingly erratic in its course, yet true to its nature and controlled by fixed immutable laws, startling and awing the observer or challenging respect and admiration. Such organize and decree success and distinction in obedience to the laws of mind, not only by unremitting effort and toil even, but by a wise adjustment of means to ends, having regard to principles as definite and undeviating in their applications as those which guide the chemist in the laboratory, the physician at the bedside, and the surgeon in the operating hall. Their success is not the result of accident, 'luck,' unusual mental endowments, aid of friends, but rather the legitimate and necessary sequence of industry, perseverance, energy, clearness of perception, oneness of purpose, fixedness of effort, and strength of will.

If the circumstances and surroundings are not favorable, no energies are squandered in useless hesitancy or unmanly murmurings, but are modified, and, if possible, made subservient to the great purpose of life, or may be utterly ignored : while the aspiring candidate for distinction and an enviable pre-eminence determines never for a moment to entertain the idea of 'a cessation of hostilities'—never admits into his vocabulary the word fail."

Junius Henri Brown defines genius as an inexhaustible capacity to labor and a tireless patience to perform. Shelley, Byron, Agassiz, Darwin, Edison, Gould—what were they, what have they been but tremendous, unremitting, patient workers? What records would Dickens, Macaulay, Beecher, have left but for their zeal for labor, their ceaseless energy in doing? It was not that these or any of them were nursed in the lap of luxury that they waxed strong. It was to no adventitious aids of circumstance that they owed success. They wrought their greatness out of the mighty forces that opposed them; their monuments are builded of stones which they lifted and placed with their own strong hands.

POVERTY NO BARRIER.

Success is for him who conquers it. It yields only to masterful endeavor. George Peabody began life poor; his education was meager, yet riches, honor, a deathless fame were his achievements. You, young man, perhaps you despair because your field of opportunity seems narrow. Yet it is boundless. You falter because you think yourself handicapped by poverty. Yet poverty was no bar to the ambition of Lincoln, Stewart, Greeley, Childs, Garfield. You hesitate to adventure toward the heights because you fancy that only those may reach them who have the inspiration of the classics. Yet it is the testimony of the successful merchants, bankers, railway magnates and manufacturers of Chicago and other cities, that colleges are not always a help to those who undertake a business career. To one who wishes to command success in the ordinary walks of life, in merchandising, banking, manufacturing, speculating, a common school education is not only ample, it is the best. To go through college is to lose valuable time. To study the classics is to load the mind with material that can be of no possible use in the practical affairs of the counting-house and factory. For these the common English branches, as they are taught in the city or the village high school, meet the full requirement; and every day spent outside of these is a day lost so far as advancement in business pursuits is concerned.

· You have no reason to despond. The future is yours to command. The road to success lies before you, and if you foot it bravely every obstacle will yield.

> "In the world's broad field of battle,
>   In the bivouac of life,
> Be not like dumb, driven cattle;
>   Be a hero in the strife.
>
> Trust no future, howe'er pleasant;
>   Let the dead Past bury its dead.
> Act, act in the living Present,
>   Heart within and God o'erhead.

BOYS.

Lives of great men all remind us
  We can make our lives sublime,
And, departing, leave behind us
  Footprints on the sands of time,—

Footprints that perhaps another,
  Sailing o'er Life's solemn main,—
A forlorn and shipwrecked brother,—
  Seeing, shall take heart again.

Let us, then, be up and doing,
  With a heart for any fate;
Still achieving, still pursuing,
  Learn to labor and to wait."

GIRLS.

Girlhood.

GIRLS.

"By what glow and melody of speech," exclaimed Horace Mann, "can I sketch the vision of a young and beautiful daughter, with all her bewildering enchantments? By what cunning art can the coarse material of words be refined and subtleized into color and motion and music, till they shall paint the bloom of health, 'celestial, rosy red;' till they shall trace those motions that have the grace and the freedom of flame, and echo the sweet and affectionate tones of a spirit yet warm from the hand that created it? What less than a divine power could have strung the living chords of her voice to pour out unbidden and exulting harmonies? What fount of sacred flame kindles and feeds the light that gleams from the pure depths of her eye, and flushes her cheek with the hues of a perpetual morning, and shoots auroras from her beaming forehead? O, profane not this last miracle of heavenly workmanship with sight or sound of earthly impurity!

"Keep vestal vigils around her inborn modesty; and let the quickest lightnings blast her tempter. She is nature's mosaic of charms. Looked upon as we look upon an object of natural history—upon a gazelle or a hyacinth—she is a magnet to draw pain out of a wounded breast. While we gaze upon her, and press her in ecstasy to our bosom, we almost tremble,, lest suddenly she should unfurl a wing and soar to some better world."

A MOTHER'S RESPONSIBILITY.

No heavier responsibility is placed upon the mother than that involved in the training of a daughter. Her boy needs her love and her watchful care and sweet instruction, it is true, and every man will trace most that is good and noble and pure in him to his mother; but how infinitely greater is the daughter's need of a mother's gentle influences and pure example! How infinitely more tender the plant that is to blossom into womanhood than that which matures into sturdy self-protecting, self-asserting and self-sustaining manhood. A boy's will is the wind's will, according to the poet's song, but the girl's will—ah! how different it is! How soft and compliant, how yielding to all outward pressure, how susceptible to the sweet influences of mother-love. how docile and tractable!

Yet too often the young girl grows up like a neglected flower. Too often she is suffered to run wild amid influences that contaminate and through scenes that leave an ugly and indelible impress upon her soul. She knows much that she never ought to know; much that she should be taught she never learns. Her mother is a busy woman and she trusts the school to train her daughter for womanhood. The girl becomes estranged; the mother is no longer her confidant, but she confides in some one and goes there for consolation, advice and instruction. Who knows what instruction and advice she will receive? Who knows what a careless word or an evil suggestion may not do? Who shall say what temptations may be thrown in her way, what perils may beset her path, what vicious counsels may threaten the temple where purity and innocence are enshrined? Certainly her mother's duty here is one of the deepest solemnity. Her boy may take care of himself. He may be wild and reckless in youth; but one day there will come a change. His manhood will assert itself and he will settle down to the serious business of life with resolute purpose and lofty determination. But his sister! What of her? Shall she follow the wind? Shall she seek her own companions and pursue her own devices unchecked? Shall she be trusted to tread the paths of youth and inexperience without a guide? Nay, not so. For one breath of the north wind can destroy the fairest garden, so one touch of evil upon a young girl's life is fatal. Her brother may survive and indeed be strengthened in his moral fibers by contact with the grosser realities of the world, but she, delicate, fragile, tender as she is, she can no more withstand the blighting, blasting effects of suspicion or scandal than a rose-leaf can withstand a nipping frost.

Fortunately for the race, fortunately for the peace and tranquility of domestic life, mother-duty is not always neglected. Indeed, it is the rare case, after all, which is marked by indifference or thoughtlessness on the part of the mother in the training of her daughter, and let us thank God that it is so. But the misfortune is, the pity is, that there is any sweet flower left to bloom among the weeds and mingle its delicate perfume with the foul odors of a neglected home. It is sad to think that any of God's shining vessels are destined to pollution; and every instinct of love should urge us to a higher sense of the responsibility that is imposed by mother-hood and fatherhood. It is a fearful yet a precious and glorious responsibility. To shirk it is not only unnatural but criminal. To slight it or depreciate it is a sad and grievious mistake. To live up to the full measure of it is to earn a distinction of the noblest and most enduring nature.

TAKE YOUR DAUGHTER INTO YOUR CONFIDENCE.

Mothers in these days are sometimes too lenient with their daughters in certain respects. It is bad to restrain a girl too much, to make her feel that her liberty is taken away or threatened; but her wilder impulses may be curbed, her wayward steps guided, without leaving upon her mind the sense of injustice. A mother ought to take her young girl into her confidence. She ought to teach her by precept and example. No secrets should stand as bars between them. The girl should be made to feel that her best, her truest, her readiest and most sympathetic friend is her mother. In every stage of her development the girl needs watching, caution, help, admonition, advice and the lights of larger experience. These the mother must supply if she would not have her daughter waver in her course and perhaps wander from it. She needs support and guidance, but not espionage and tyranny. Many a good girl has been spoiled by ill-considered re-striction and cruel distrust. She has grown rebellious under treatment which outraged her finer sensibilities; and when either girls or boys rebel there is no answering for what they will do.

CHAPERONS.

The old duenna system of Spain, Italy and France, a survival of which we see in the fashionable chaperon of to-day, was well meant, we doubt not, and possibly it may have had its uses, but there is nothing in the moral history of those countries, nothing in their social records to vindicate the wisdom or the justice of a tyrannous surveillance of young girls. Indeed, there is every reason to infer from that history and those records that, so far from the system having subserved the purposes of virtue, it was an incentive to intrigue and a worse than futile bar against gallantry.

TEACH THEM SELF-RELIANCE.

Girls thus hedged about lacked self-reliance; and it was but human nature for them to rebel against a slavery to custom and parental authority. English girls were freer; their range was greatly larger; their social restraints were far less severe; yet no one will contend that they were less pure and virtuous than their Spanish and Italian sisters. Nay, the fact is, that the standard of morality in England was never so low as that in either Spain or Italy; and here in America, where young women are granted greater freedom than anywhere else in the world, the moral standard is high, and woman is everywhere respected and reverenced. Her self-reliance is strong, her faith in herself abiding, her conscious innocence a stronger shield than ever duenna was against the breath of scandal.

No. Girls do not require espionage; they need friendly and sympathetic counsel, and above all, wholesome example. It will be very hard for that girl who has an evil-disposed mother to become a really good woman. A bad pattern will be before her all the time and unconsciously she will weave it into the warp and woof of her own character. Sadee, the Persian poet, beautifully depicts the influence of environment in this simple apologue: "One day as I was in the bath, a friend of mine put into my hand a piece of scented clay. I took it and said to it, 'Art thou musk or ambergris, for I am charmed with thy perfume?' It answered, 'I was a despicable piece of clay, but I was some time in the company of the rose; the sweet quality of my companion was communicated to me, otherwise I should be only a bit of clay, as I appear to be.'"

Thus a sweet and pure-hearted mother may by her example and her gentle influences do more to restrain a wayward girl, imparting to her nature the perfume of her own, than convent walls and spying eyes; and we would impress this truth, for it is a truth, upon every mother who reads this book.

A GIRL'S DUTY TO HER MOTHER AND HOME.

At the same time we would impress upon the daughter herself the duty she owes to the mother, to society and to her own womanhood. The responsibility is not all with the parents. Some of it rests upon the girl herself and she must not

⸮ek to evade nor must she dispute it. She owes her mother not only affection and respect, but confidence and cheerful help in all domestic affairs. It is not enough that a young lady should sing and play and dance well; she should be able likewise to sew and cook well. She should know how to darn a stocking as well as how to paint a panel. And she should not forget that there is quite as fine (and perhaps a nobler) art in baking a loaf of good bread or making a cake as there is in rendering a Beethoven sonata. It is said that the French girl is devoted to music because she loves; but when she is married her piano is forgotten and her husband and home become the center of all her activities and aspirations. She puts as much soul in her cookery as she once threw into her music; and the pot replaces the piano as the means of expressing the poetry and passion of her nature.

FREQUENTLY ONLY ORNAMENTAL.

The modern young woman is too frequently a mere ornament. She knows nothing of any great consequence and is as helpless as an infant in domestic affairs. She cannot sew, she cannot cook, her notions of household economy are vague, and if she were called to be the mistress of a home she would be the victim of her servants and a burden upon her husband. No girl, no matter what the wealth and position of her family, should be permitted to grow up so. Every girl should be trained and carefully trained, in domestic management. She should know the value of a dollar and how to spend it to the very best advantage. It may be that fortune may always smile upon her and that she may never be actually required to work and save, yet the chances of life are hazardous and it is always prudent to provide for emergencies.

STERLING WORTH.

With the average girl, however, it is not a question of providing against remote chances. She is not the daughter of wealth and in the nature of things must ultimately face the world with very little except her own personal qualities and accomplishments. Her hand will not be sought because of its deftness in touching the keys or in handling the pencil and brush. It will be striven for rather because its owner is known to be trained in the duties of home—for it is a home that man wants; and he doesn't get that when he weds a woman who is merely ornamental, so far as accomplishments go.

This may sound very prosaic and unromantic, and perhaps it is so; but it is none the less true and none the less important. The mother owes it to her daughter and the daughter owes it to herself to take account of practical things. The real serious business of life must be considered, and frills and flourishes may be more safely neglected than those solid details of every-day household economy upon which so much depends.

"It is the paradise of marriage," says Michelet, "that the man shall work for the woman; that he alone shall support her, take pleasure in enduring fatigue for her sake, and spare her the hardships of labor, and rude contact with the world."

Mother and Daughter.

"He returns home in the evening, harassed, suffering from toil, mental or bodily, from the weariness of worldly things, from the baseness of men. But in his reception at home there is such an infinite kindness, a calm so intense, that he hardly believes in the cruel realities he has gone through all the day. 'No,' he says, 'that could not have been; it was but an ugly dream. There is but one real thing in the world, and that is you!'

"This is woman's mission . . . to renew the heart of man. Protected and nourished by the man, she in turn nourishes him with her love.

"In love is her true sphere of labor, the only labor that it is essential she should perform. It was that she should reserve herself entirely for this that nature made her so incapable of performing the ruder sorts of earthly toil.

"Man's business it is to earn money, her's to spend it: that is to say, *to regulate household expenditures* better than man would.

"This renders him indifferent to all enjoyment that is bought, and makes it seem to him insipid. Why should he go elsewhere in search of pleasure? What pleasure is there apart from the woman he loves?

"It is well said in Eastern law, that 'the wife is the household.' And better still said the Eastern poet: 'A wife is a fortune.'

"Our Western experience enables us to add: 'Especially when she is poor.'

"Then, though she has nothing, she brings you every-thing."

It is a defect of our civilization that women are forced to become bread-winners. Young girls who ought to be training in the school at home for the high and holy duties of wifehood and motherhood are compelled by social and industrial maladjustments to enter the hurly-burly of the great work-a-day world, competing with those who ought to support them in the desperate struggle for existence, every year, it seems, growing more fierce. This is sad and terrible and the condition may well arrest the attention and excite the apprehension of the thoughtful. What will be the out-come time alone can tell, but this is clear, that it is a bad school, that of the factory and workshop, to which so many girls are sent by circumstance, in that formative time when the mother's influence is most needed and domestic suscep-tibilities are keenest. Yet the situation is one that cannot be blinded. It confronts many thousands of families and it cannot be easily escaped, if it is possible to escape it at all; so it comes to this, that they must make the best of it, mothers and daughters alike, the one giving what instruction they can, the others acquiring such knowledge and facility as they may in those domestic arts which make home the hope and the haven that it is.

COURTSHIP.

Love is strong as death. Many waters cannot quench love,
neither can the floods drown it.—*Proverbs.*

Love rules the court, the camp, the grove,
And men below, and saints above;
For love is heaven, and heaven is love.
Scott: "Lay of the Last Minstrel."

COURTSHIP.

Love is the universal passion. It burns alike in the heart of the prince and peasant. Soldier and statesman, poet and plowman, sage and simple, all yield to its masterful sway. And he that loves carries with him in his breast some fragment of paradise. Shelley says that "all love is sweet, given or returned. Common as light is love, and its familiar voice wearies not ever. They who inspire it most are fortunate; but those who feel it most are happier still." Shakespeare had a very poor opinion of the woman-hater. "He that feels no love for woman," said he, "is foe to all the finer feelings of the soul; and to sweet Nature's holiest, tenderest ties a heartless renegade." And the poet Crabbe thought it "better to love amiss, than nothing to have loved." Sheridan believed the divine passion to be no monopoly of man. Even an oyster, he held, may be crossed in love. Southey sang that "love is indestructible; its holy flame forever burneth; from heaven it came, to heaven returneth." Lord Lytton declared that "love, like death, levels all ranks, and lays the shepherd's crook beside the sceptre." And what is love? Who can describe it? Who can say how it comes or interpret all its various meanings? Scott sings of true love thus:

"True love the gift which God has given
To man alone beneath the heaven:
It is not fantasy's hot fire,

> Whose wishes, soon as granted, fly;
> It lieth not in fierce desire,
> With dead desire it doth not die;
> It is the secret sympathy,
> The silver link, the silken tie,
> Which heart to heart, and mind to mind,
> In body and in soul can bind."

Life is a silent harp until touched by the finger of love. It then thrills with harmonies of heaven. Till this awakening all has been a dreamy joyous existence in the fairyland of home. A mother's affection has guided and guarded you, but now you are about to start in life for yourself, and the golden chain of love binds your heart to another heart, thus fulfilling the law of your being. It is an honor to you, young men, that you possess the love and confidence of an affectionate woman; and to you, young women, it should be a matter of pride that a true man's heart has been laid at your feet.

CHOOSING A MATE.

The period of mating is one of the most important in the life of the young. Nay, it is the most important, for upon the choice which each makes in this great business depends all the future. It is so easy to make a mistake and so hard to correct it, once made.

Courting is not a science to be studied in books, but there is an art in it—the art of pleasing. Anciently, talismans and charms were relied on by youth and maiden; "but is now many years since the only talismans for creating love are the charms of the person beloved." By gracefully displaying those advantages conferred by nature, and by assiduously cultivating the graces that art can bestow, every man may hope to win a mate and every maid may lead captive a lover. And in this field, moral qualities at least count for more than physical; and while few men are endowed with those attractions of form and face which are sometimes successful, all may hope to acquire those elements of character, understanding and manners, which more often command the esteem and win the love of women. Colley Cibber expresses the common judgment of the fair sex in this matter when he puts in the mouth of one of his women the sentiment that "the only merit of a man is his sense, while doubtless the greatest value of a woman is her beauty." Beauty is certainly the master-charm of the softer sex, and it is felt to be so by themselves. Yet while we observe its power and its value we must not lose sight of its dangers. Woman's charms are often her ruin, and what she makes her boast is not infrequently her curse.

MANHOOD AND WOMANHOOD THE BASIS.

Manhood and womanhood should be the basis of matrimonial choice. Old Themistocles said: "If compelled to choose, I would bestow my daughter upon a man without money, sooner than upon money without a man." When Dr. Franklin was asked why he was always so happy he said: "It is no secret; I have got one of the best of wives; when I go to work, she always has a kind word of encouragement for me, and when I come home, she meets me with a smile and a kiss, and the tea is sure to be ready, and she has done so many things through the day to please me, that I cannot find it in my heart to speak an unkind word to anybody." Thus souls properly mated are constantly falling in love with each other. Each day reveals some new beauty to admire and sorrows come only to chasten and to bind them closer together.

MARRIED PEOPLE MEET ADVERSITY BEST.

"I have noticed," said Washington Irving, "that a married man falling into misfortune is more apt to retrieve his situation than a single one, chiefly because his spirits are softened and relieved by domestic endearments, and self-respect kept alive by finding that, although all abroad be darkness and humiliation, yet still there is a little world of love at home of which he is monarch; whereas a single man is apt to run to waste and self-neglect, to fall to ruin, like a deserted mansion, for want of inhabitants. Those disasters which break down the spirit of man and prostrate him in the dust, seem to call forth all the energies of the gentler sex, and to give such intrepidity and elevation to their character that at times it approaches to sublimity." And Bishop Taylor says regarding the influences of a good wife: "If you are for pleasure, marry; if you prize rosy health, marry. A good wife is Heaven's last and best gift to man, his angel of mercy. Her voice is his sweetest music; her smile his brightest day; her kiss the guardian of his innocence; her industry his surest wealth; her economy his safest steward; her lips his faithful counselors; her bosom his safest pillow; her prayer his ablest advocate at Heaven's court."

Courtship.

CHOOSE JUDICIOUSLY.

But while all this is true, while a happy union is the source of prosperity and strength, it is not less true that an unfortunate marriage is destructive alike of human happiness and hopes. It is thus of the very highest importance that the choice of a life-partner shall be made wisely. Upon the discretion you exercise in this great matter depends your future and there is no business of your life which demands greater prudence or more prayerful consideration. With the lady this choice is only negative. She may love, but she must not declare her passion; she can but wait. When the time comes, it is her prerogative to accept or decline, but until the lover speaks, she must remain silent and passive. That this often involves a great trial of her patience who can doubt? That it sometimes cruelly affects her peace and happiness who will deny?

With the man the case is different. It is his prerogative to woo and his to declare his love. He may speak and learn his fate when he will, and in this is his great advantage. Being refused, he may go elsewhere to seek his mate, if that be his humor, and it will be his own fault if he fails to find her.

BE CIRCUMSPECT.

But a gentleman should be at all times circumspect and considerate in his attentions to the opposite sex. In no case should he devote himself exclusively to one lady unless he is thinking seriously of marriage. He may call upon all and extend invitations to any or all to attend places of amusement

6

with him without compromise, but the moment he neglects others to devote himself to a particular lady, that moment he gives the favored one reason to attach a serious importance to his attentions. Her feelings may very naturally become engaged and if he should not be in earnest a great deal of mischief may be done—her happiness may be destroyed.

Nor should a lady allow any marked attention from one toward whom she is indifferent. In the first place, as a true woman she cannot take the risk of inflicting a wound she cannot heal. She must deal honorably with her admirers, and judiciously avoid the encouragement of a suit she cannot accept. In the first place she owes it to herself to discourage an undesirable suitor that she may not injure herself by keeping aloof from those she might prefer. If it should appear that her feelings are already interested in the one, the others will be slow to approach and may indeed leave her altogether. Before tolerating the serious addresses of any man a woman should feel that it will be possible in time to return his affections, measure for measure. It lies with the man to propose, but the prerogative of refusing is woman's and this prerogative a lady of tact and kind heart can and will exercise before her suitor is brought to the humiliation of an open declaration. She may let him see that she accepts the attentions of others with equal favor and she may kindly, yet firmly check his too frequent visits. But while discouraging him as a lover she should try to retain him as a friend, and this she may do by an open and honorable course.

BE NOT HASTY.

The young man who makes a proposal of marriage to a young lady on brief acquaintance is not only indiscreet but presumptuous. He may have no doubt of her merits, but how can he fancy himself so irresistible as to suppose her equally satisfied ? A woman who would accept a gentleman at first sight can hardly possess that discretion needed in a good wife and we therefore counsel the impetuous lover to restrain his ardor, thus avoiding the chances of disappointment. Discretion is as wise in love as it is in war.

LOVE AT FIRST SIGHT.

That there is no such a thing as "love at first sight" is hardly to be questioned. Indeed Marlow goes so far as to ask "Who ever loved that loved not at first sight?" But love alone is a very uncertain foundation upon which to base wedlock. There should be something more than love between a man and woman before they venture upon the sea of matrimony. There ought to be a thorough acquaintance, a harmony of tastes and temperament and a deep-rooted esteem. Without these their ship will be without ballast and the waves may make a wreck of it before it fairly enters upon the long life voyage.

THE COQUETTE.

It is a melancholy fact that some young women pride themselves upon their conquests, regardless of the mischief they have done to those whose hearts they have cruelly wounded. It is a shameful vanity, and no true woman will indulge in it. Hers is a poor triumph who can say, or feel, that she has refused five, ten or twenty offers of marriage. She does little more, indeed, than acknowledge herself a trifler and coquette, who, from motives of personal vanity, tempts and induces hopes and expectations which she knows she will disappoint.

But if her course is unprincipled and immodest, what shall we say of the man who plays with the affections of a woman? If the female trifler is cruel, is not the male coquette almost criminal? He conveys the impression, that he is in love by actions, gallantries, looks, attentions, all—except that he never commits himself—and finally withdraws, exulting in the thought that he has said or written nothing which can be held legally binding. Upon such a man the world rightly looks with the severest reprobation and his course is one which every honorable representative of the sterner sex will studiously avoid.

BE FRANK AND HONEST.

A woman of considerate feelings will not keep a lover in suspense. When she sees clearly that she has become the object of his especial regard, and she does not wish to encourage his addresses, she will take the earliest opportunity offering to make known the state of her mind. She will not be harsh, but generous and humane. A refined ease of manner will satisfy him, if he have any discernment, that his suit is hopeless. Should her natural disposition render this difficut, let her deliberately show that she wishes

to avoid his company, and he will presently withdraw. If
this should fail let her allow an opportunity for explanation
to occur. She can then speak decisively, yet kindly, with
the assurance that, if he be a man of good judgment and
right feeling, he will trouble her no further. But let it never
be said of her that she permitted the attentions of an honorable man when she had no heart to give him. It may be
that his preference has been gratifying and his conversation
delightful. Her vanity may have been flattered by the devotion of one her companions admire. She may really have a
doubt in her own mind as to the true state of her feelings.
Yet all this will not excuse her. She ought to know her own
heart and she will not be held guiltless if she trifle with that
of another.

THE REJECTED SUITOR.

Nor, after rejecting a suitor, will she be held guiltless
should she betray the fact. The secret does not belong to
her, and if she possess either generosity or gratitude for offered affection, she will guard it jealously. It is sufficiently
painful to be refused without incurring the added mortifica-
tion of being pointed out as a rejected lover.

When a man has proffered his hand in marriage and it
has been refused, his duty is quite clear. Etiquette demands
that he shall accept the lady's decision as final and retire
from the field. He has no right to demand the reason of her
refusal. Should she give it, he is bound in honor to respect
her secret, if it be a secret, and hold it inviolable. To persist in urging his suit or to follow up the lady with marked

attentions would be in the worst possible taste. His only proper course is to withdraw as much as possible from the circle which she adorns, thus sparing her all embarrassment and himself a great deal of unnecessary anguish.

Rejected suitors somtimes act on the theory that they have sustained injuries which they are bound to avenge, and so miss no chance to annoy and slight the helpless victims of their former gallantries. Such conduct is both cruel and cowardly. The manly man will never adopt a course so indefensible, and he writes himself down as a puppy who permits his spite to show itself against a woman.

DO NOT PROVOKE LOVERS' QUARRELS.

When a young lady encourages the addresses of a young man, she should behave honorably and sensibly. She should not lead him about as if in triumph, nor take advantage of her ascendancy over him by playing with his feelings, She should not seek for occasions to tease him, that she may try his temper. Neither should she affect indifference, nor provoke a lovers' quarrel for the foolish pleasure of reconciliation. On her conduct during the period of courtship will largely depend the estimation in which her husband will hold her in after life. No hard and fast rule can be laid down regarding the form of an avowal of love.

PROPOSING.

It is probable that every lover, before he makes his passion known, exercises his fancy in the formation of some pretty or eloquent phrase for conveying the tremendous secret that masters his heart; but where one lover remembers his fine speech at the critical moment, perhaps a hundred will forget and make the disclosure in words altogether unmeditated. If the declaration is made by letter, there is, of course, a wide field open for eloquence, but this should always be tempered by good sense, and a degree of moderation. Every allusion to the lady should be marked with respect, and the proposal should be in clear, simple and honest words, whose power will be in their candor and sincerity. As a general thing, however, proposals should be made by word of mouth. They may not thus be couched in such graceful and poetic language, but they will borrow an eloquence which mere words cannot express from the presence of the beloved, and the inspiration of her eyes, her smile, her touch.

Perhaps Dickens, in "David Copperfield," has furnished the best formula for a proposal. It was merely "Barkis is willin'," and served every purpose. Peggoty understood, and that was quite sufficient.

Trollope says on this subject: "We are inclined to think that these matters are not always discussed by mortal lovers in the poetically passionate phraseology which is generally thought to be appropriate. A man cannot well describe that which he has never seen or heard, but the absolute words and acts of one such scene did once come to the author's knowledge. The couple were by no means plebeian, or below the proper standard of high bearing and high breeding. They were a handsome pair, living among educated people, sufficiently given to mental pursuits, and in every way what a pair of polite lovers ought to be. The all-important conversation passed in this wise. The site of the passionate scene was the sea-shore, on which they were walking, in autumn.

"Gentleman—'Well, miss, the long and short of it is this: Here I am; you can take me or leave me.'

"Lady (scratching a gutter on the sand with her parasol, so as to allow a little salt water to run out of one hole into another)—'Of course I know that's all nonsense.'

"Gentleman—'Nonsense! By Jove! It isn't nonsense at all! Come, Jane, here I am; come, at any rate you can say something.'

"Lady—'Yes, I suppose I can say something.'

"Gentleman—'Well, which is it to be—take me or leave me?'

"Lady (very slowly, and with a voice, perhaps, hardly articulate, carrying on at the same time her engineering works on a wider scale)—'Well, I don't exactly want to leave you.'

"And so the matter was settled; settled with much propriety and satisfaction, and both the lady and gentleman would have thought, had they ever thought about the matter at all, that this, the sweetest moment of their lives, had been graced by all the poetry by which such moments ought to be hallowed."

CONSULTING HER PARENTS.

The proposal over and the lady's acceptance secured, the next thing is to "see papa." And here is an ordeal that will test the courage of the boldest lover. If you have not had the experience, you can scarcely conjecture what it is to stand in the presence of your Mary's father and mother, and ask them for her hand in marriage. Just how to approach the momentous question gracefully is a thing that can hardly be told. The old folks will not be looking at your suit from the sentimental side. They will take the practical view, and it will behoove you, therefore, to bear this fact in mind. If you shift from one foot to the other, fidgeting a good deal, and giving your hat a closer inspection than it ever had be. fore, while your heart thumps like a trip-hammer, and your tongue becomes unmanageable, console yourself, if you can, with the reflection that the stern father who now confronts you so coolly, and it may be with such an air of superiority, has himself faced a like ordeal: and then plunge desperately into the midst of your subject. You may not be very coherent, and possibly you will be quite ridiculous, viewed from the strictly critical standpoint; but never mind, the old folks will understand, and make all necessary allowances. You will have been eloquent and explicit enough if you have simply said: "Can Mary be my wife?" Of course, if you are cooler, and have the necessary self-command, you may describe to the parents the state of your affections, hinting as you pass that Mary is not altogether indifferent, and then pass naturally and frankly to the main question which will concern them, namely, your resources and prospects in life. If you can give a satisfactory proof of your ability to provide for Mary and a possible family, their consent to your marriage will scarcely be withheld if you are otherwise worthy. A newspaper anecdote is recalled in this connection :

"How much property have you?" inquired a careful father of the young man who had asked for his daughter's hand.

"None," replied the suitor. "But I am chuck full of days' work."

He got the girl. And it is probably true that all sensible fathers would sooner bestow their daughters upon industrious and energetic young men who are not afraid of days' work, than upon idle loungers with fortunes at their command.

THE ENGAGEMENT RING.

When the engagement has been duly made and ratified, it is customary for the young man to seal the compact by some present to his affianced. A ring is the usual form of the gift, and it may be as costly as the gentleman's means will justify, Among the wealthy the preference is for diamonds, and either a solitaire or a cluster ring may be chosen. But the ring may be set with any other stone—the diamond is not essential—or it may be a family heirloom, precious on account of its associations, its antiquity, or its quaintness, rather than by reason of its intrinsic value. The engagement ring should be worn upon the ring finger of the right hand.

CONDUCT DURING ENGAGEMENT.

After the engagement the young man acquires a proper standing as a member of the family. He should be recognized as such, and the family of the engaged lady should endeavor to make her suitor feel at home, however protracted his visits may be.

As to the length of engagements, that, of course, is a matter which each couple must settle for themselves, according to circumstances. But protracted engagements, as a rule, are to be avoided; they are universally embarrassing. Lovers are prone to grow exacting, jealous and morose.

> "Alas ! how slight a cause can move
> Dissension between hearts that love."

Yet, if neither should assume a masterful or jealous attitude toward the other, the course of their true love may run quite smooth. It were well that they go about in society very much after their engagement as they went before. They should not shut themselves away from the rest of the world, and the fact that they have confessed their love to each other ought to be a sufficient guaranty of fidelity. For the rest, let there be trust and confidence.

The attitudé of engaged couples toward each other should be frank, yet delicate, warm, yet restrained. A lady will not be too demonstrative of her affection during the interesting period of her engagement. "There's many a slip 'twixt the cup and the lip," and overt displays of passion are not pleasant to remember by a young lady if the man in the case by any chance fails to become her husband. An honorable man will never tempt his future bride to any such demonstrations. He will never forget to treat her with due respect, and maintain a chivalrous decorum in his demeanor toward her.

"Lovers hours are long, though seeming short," says the bard of Avon. If so easy to forget the flight of time in the presence of the one we love, yet lovers should not be unmindful of the real pain and inconvenience they occasion the objects of their devotion when they keep them up beyond a reasonable hour, subjecting them to ridicule and censure of others.

In passing, it may be remarked that it is not improper to leave an engaged couple alone sometimes, but that they should be always so left, under all circumstances and at no matter what inconvenience to others, is as absurd as it is indelicate.

THE DOMINEERING LOVER.

The lover who assumes a domineering attitude over his future wife invites her to escape from his tyranny while yet she may, and if she be wise she will escape, for the chances are that he will be worse as a husband than as a lover.

BROKEN ENGAGEMENTS.

When an engagement is to be broken, as engagements must be sometimes, owing to the appearance of circumstances which make the fulfillment of the compact undesirable, it is best to do the necessarily painful work by letter. It is a serious business and it should be undertaken in a serious spirit. The position of the acting party is delicate and embarrassing and both tact and generous forbearance should be exercised. The letter should be calm and explicit. A clear and fair statement of the reasons for breaking the engagement should be given and no room left for doubt. The communication should be conclusive, yet gentle, and when sent should be accompanied by everything in the way of portraits, letters or gifts, which have been received during the engagement. When such a letter has been received it should be acknowledged with dignity and without reproach. No effort should be made or measures taken to reverse the decision, unless it is obviously founded on a mistake or a misapprehension. In that case, proof of the true situation should be made, that harmony may be restored and the old relations re-established more firmly than ever. But if the reason justify the act, then there is no room for argument or expostulation. There is nothing to be done but to accept the decision and return whatever has been received in the way of gifts, letters and pictures.

WEDDINGS.

Not for the summer-hour alone,
  When skies resplendent shine;
And youth and pleasure fill the throne,
  Our hearts and hands we twine;
But for those stern and wintry days
  Of peril, pain and fear,
When Heaven's wise discipline doth make
  The earthly journey drear.

—Mrs. Sigourney.

WEDDINGS.

The institution of marriage is everywhere, among civilized men, the most regarded. Empires may fall, dynasties disappear, states crumble and constitutions fall to pieces, yet this sacred compact, this solid foundation of the family and guaranty of social order, remains the one enduring factor in societies that would otherwise lapse into barbarism and end in ruin.

And marriage is the secret dream, the inspiring hope, of every heart. Even Benedick yielded at last; and never yet was there man or woman so embittered in soul that no sweet thought lingered of home and children and domestic joys.

Marriage is, indeed, the great business of life. Our poetry, our romance, our drama, the fine arts, all find their chief inspiration in the divine passion that knits lives together and sets up the fireside trinity under every roof. Young men in the factory, the field and the counting-house find joy in their toil because it brings nearer to them the realization of their highest hope. Young women at school or at home dream of the sacred mysteries of love and silently prepare themselves for the great mission which is theirs to fulfill.

RITES AND CEREMONIES.

Marriage is a solemn event and it is appropriately marked by rites and ceremonies befitting its sacred character.

These vary with the fortunes and wishes of the interested parties, the groom usually deferring to the bride in all such matters. The form of the rite of marriage may be studied by Methodists in their "Book of Discipline;" by Episcopalians in their "Book of Common Prayer," and by Catholics in their "Ritual." In most cases a rehearsal of the ceremony is made in private, in order to avoid awkward blunders at the altar. If the wedding takes place before a magistrate, the ceremony is merely nominal. The Catholic and Episcopalian forms are the most elaborate and perhaps the most impressive, but the simplest form is equally effectual. The following rules are generally received as governing in this momentous and interesting conjuncture:

When the wedding is not strictly private, it is customary for bridesmaids and groomsmen to be chosen to assist in the duties of the occasion.

BRIDESMAIDS.

The bridesmaids should be younger than the bride; their dresses should be conformed to hers; they should not be more expensive, though they are permitted more ornament. Some light, graceful material for such dresses is usually selected, and flowers are the principal decoration.

The bride's dress is marked by its simplicity. But few jewels or ornaments should be worn, and these should be the gift either of the bridegroom or the parents. A veil and garland are the distinguishing features of the bride's costume.

The bridesmaids assist in dressing the bride, receiving the company, etc. During the ceremony they stand at the bride's left, the first bridesmaid holding the bride's bouquet and gloves.

GROOMSMEN.

The groomsmen receive the clergyman, present him to the couple to be married, and support the bridegroom upon the right during the ceremony.

CONGRATULATIONS.

If the wedding takes place in the evening, at home, immediately after the ceremony the happy pair are congratulated, first by the relatives, then by the friends, after which they are at liberty to mingle with the company. The dresses, supper, etc., are usually more gay and elaborate than for a morning wedding and reception, where the friends stop for a few moments, only, to congratulate the newly-married pair, taste the cake and wine, and hurry away.

CHURCH WEDDING.

When the ceremony takes place in church, the bride enters at the left, with her father, mother, and bridesmaids; or, at all events, with a bridesmaid. The groom enters at the right, followed by his attendants. The parents stand behind, the attendants at either side.

The bride should be certain that her glove is readily removable; the groom that the ring is where he can find it; otherwise delay and embarrassment may occur.

In leaving the church, bride and groom walk arm-in-arm. Usually a two-hours' reception follows at home, their intimate friends being present, and partaking of the wedding breakfast.   If the lady appears at the breakfast, which is certainly desirable, she occupies, with her husband, the center of the table, and sits by his side, her father and mother taking the top and bottom, showing all honor to their guests.   When the cake has been cut, and the health of bride and groom has been duly drunk, the bride, attended by her friends, withdraws, and, when ready for her departure, the newly-wedded pair start on their wedding journey, generally about 2 or 3 o'clock, the rest of the company shortly after taking their leave.

On such a festive occasion, all appear in their best attire and assume their best manners.   As stranger guests may be present, care should be taken lest the good breeding of the family be compromised by some neglect in small things. Mysteries concerning knives, forks and plates, or throwing "an old shoe" after the bride, have long been exploded, and are highly reprehensible. Such practices may seem immaterial, but they are not so, and they should be studiously avoided.

WEDDING CARDS.

Wedding cards are usually sent out to friends and relatives, designating the date and hour when the newly married pair will be "at home." In some circles these cards are issued almost immediately after the ceremony, but as some little inconvenience occasionally attends this custom, as young people may wish to extend their wedding tour, or since unavoidable delays may occur in a long journey, it is perhaps better to postpone sending cards for a short time at least.

The Corsican Wedding.

As fashions, in wedding cards, change as frequently and capriciously as fashions in bonnets, it were idle to say more on the subject than that good taste dictates simplicity rather than ostentation. The plainer the card the more becoming and appropriate it will be as a rule.

CALLING ON NEWLY WEDDED COUPLES.

No one to whom a wedding card has not been sent ought to call on a newly wedded couple.

When the days named for seeing company arrive, remember to be punctual. If possible call the first day promptly at the designated hour. Wedding cake and wine are handed round, each guest partaking and each giving expression to some wish for the happiness of the wedded pair.

If the gentleman is in a profession, and it happens that he cannot await the arrival of such as call according to the invitation on the wedding card, an apology must be made, and, if possible, an old friend of the family should represent him. A bride must on no account receive her visitors without her mother, or sister, or some friend being present, not even if her husband is at home. This rule is imperative. To do otherwise is to disregard the usages of society.

RETURNING VISITS.

Wedding visits must be returned within the course of a few days, and parties are usually made for the young couple, which they are expected to return. However, this does not necessarily involve much visiting, neither is it expected from a young couple whose resources may be limited, or when the husband has his way to make in the world.

ADDITIONAL HINTS.

The wedding fee should be enclosed in the envelope with the marriage license. It may be any sum, from five dollars to five hundred, according to the financial ability of the bridegroom.

June is the favorite month for marriages, but September, another beautiful month in our climate, is sometimes preferred. May has been considered unlucky ever since the days of ancient Rome. Ovid says: "That time, too, was not auspicious for the marriage torches of the widow or of the virgin. She who married *then*—in May—did not long remain *a wife*."

It is left to the bride to name the day. She is also consulted in all matters of detail relating to the great event.

The wedding tour is rapidly declining in fashion. Once deemed indispensable, it is now a matter of choice, and is often not undertaken, the groom taking his bride at once to their new home, which he has prepared in advance. Nor is the honeymoon retirement any longer *de rigueur*. It may be observed or not, according to the pleasure of those most concerned.

Wedding invitations do not require any answer unless one is requested, except in the case of a sit-down breakfast, or a small home wedding. Friends at a distance acknowledge a wedding invitation by sending their cards in an envelope addressed to the bride's parents, or to the person in whose name the invitations are issued.

A recent authority says that while in England the bridesmaids may be from two to twelve in number, in this country they rarely exceed six or eight. "They should be chosen from among the sisters and other near relatives of the bride and groom, and from the bride's intimate friends. According to the present fashion, they are often dressed in picturesque, even quaint, costumes, sometimes wearing bonnets or hats, sometimes with short veils, etc. They should always wear very light colors or white." The bridesmaids should always be unmarried.

Groomsmen have been supplanted by the "best man," who usurps the functions of the former, and supports the bridegroom through all the trying ordeal. He is usually an intimate friend or a near relative of the groom, and to him is entrusted many of the small details of the affair, such as feeing the clergyman, holding the groom's hat during the ceremony, and assisting the ushers at the wedding reception.

For a daytime wedding the groom and all the gentlemen wear morning dress. The bride may wear evening dress if she pleases. The groom wears a frock coat, light trousers and gloves, but the gloves must not be white, nor must he wear a white necktie. These go only with full evening dress.

At church, the relatives of the groom are placed on the right of the altar, the relatives of the bride taking the left. The chief usher should, therefore, be acquainted with most of the relatives and guests, so that confusion in this particular may be avoided.   If, in any case he is in doubt, he may make direct inquiry of the person, and thus make sure.

Nowadays the bride usually has the ring finger of the left-hand glove cut, so that it can be readily removed, thus saving the embarrassment which once attended the removal of the whole glove.

The bride does not recognize any one in passing to or from the altar.

In the Roman Catholic Church the bride may not wear a decollette costume.

A bride does not usually dance at her own wedding, but she may join in a square dance if she chooses.

A widow, at her second marriage, does not wear orange blossoms, bridal veil or white attire.

It is now the fashion for brides to drop their middle names and substitute their family names. A widow who remarries often retains the name of her first husband as a middle name.

Wedding gifts may or may not be displayed, as the family elect.

After the wedding invitations have been issued, the bride-elect does not appear in public.

Young married people are prone to make public exhibitions of their affection. This is in exceeding bad taste and should be scrupulously avoided.

The Honeymoon.

WEDDING ANNIVERSARIES

WEDDING ANNIVERSARIES.

Anniversary weddings are now very generally celebrated and their etiquette does not widely differ from that of actual marriages. Those anniversaries which are especially observed are the fifth, the tenth, the fifteenth, the twenty-fifth and the fiftieth, the latter, it is true, occurring to very few of all those who adventure upon the sea of matrimony. On the fifth anniversary occurs what is popularly known as the wooden wedding; on the tenth the tin, on the fifteenth the crystal, on the twenty-fifth the silver and on the fiftieth the golden. The twentieth anniversary is not often celebrated, as there is a superstition, of Scotch origin, that if it is, one or the other of the married pair will die within the year.

The diamond wedding occurs on the seventy-fifth anniversary of marriage, but it is needless to say that it is very, very rarely celebrated. Other anniversaries have been named as follows, but they are not often observed in any formal manner:

Iron—the first anniversary.

Paper—the second.

Leather—the third.

Straw—the fourth.

Woolen—the seventh.

Pearl—the thirtieth.
Coral—the thirty-fifth.
Bronze—the forty-fifth.

THE INVITATIONS.

The invitations to any of these—from iron to diamond—should be appropriate in design, and the presents are expected to be in keeping. For example, cards for the pearl wedding are printed on pearl-colored board, those for coral wedding on pink and those for the bronze on bronze, while for the silver and the golden weddings, the printing is in silver and gold respectively. For the tin wedding the invitations are often on small pieces of tin-plate. enclosed in envelopes that are made in imitation of tin.

THE GOLDEN WEDDING.

The golden wedding is oftener an occasion of sad than of joyful memories. A couple who have sailed life's sea together for fifty long years must in the nature of things have left youth and hope behind them; and many wrecks must have marked their long, long voyage. Yet the golden wedding is sometimes celebrated and perhaps grandpa and grandma, surrounded by their children and their children's children, find enough in the brightness of the youth and hope around them to compensate for all the losses and disappointments of age.

THE GIFTS APPROPRIATE.

The gifts appropriate for such an occasion are suggested by the name, but it is not often that presents of gold can be afforded.   And even if they could be, it is not likely that to people who have advanced far into the valley of the shadow of death the very splendor of such rich offerings would be as a painful mockery!   It is quite sufficient that the cards announcing the event shall be done in gold on thick white paper, yet a gift of jewelry is not inappropriate.   The aged bride receives her children, grandchildren and friends in some relic of her first wedding—say the gown, or veil, or fan; and in her hand she holds a bouquet of white flowers. A wedding cake with a ring in it is prepared, the monograms of the pair, with the date of their marriage, decorating its surface.

SOMETIMES SAD.

"These golden weddings," says a recent writer, "are apt to be sad.   It is not well for the old to keep anniversaries— too many ghosts come to the feast. Still, if people are happy enough to wish to do so, there can be no harm in it.   Their surroundings may possibly surpass their fondest dreams, but as it regards themselves, the contrasts are painful. They have little in common with bridal joys, and unless it is the wish of some irrepressible descendant, few old couples care to celebrate the golden wedding save in their hearts. If they have started at the foot of the ladder and have risen, they may not wish to remember their early struggles; if they have started high and have gradually sunk into poverty or ill-health, they cer-

tainly do not wish to photograph those better days by the
fierce light of an anniversary. It is only the very exception-
ally good, happy and serene people who can afford to celebrate a golden wedding."

SILVER WEDDING.

But with the silver wedding it is very different. When
that occurs the married pair are usually in their prime. Life
is wearing the aspect of success. Perhaps the children are
all still at home, and the future smiles upon them full of
promise. The occasion is one of hope, rather than of re-
membrances and regret, and all can enter into its celebration
with cheerful zest

THE CARDS AND GIFTS.

The cards for the silver wedding are printed either on
silvered paper, or in silver ink, and the presents are all of silver, from costly dinner sets to simple ornaments. It is usual
to mark these, either with the words "Silver Wedding," or
with an appropriate motto, and the initials of the pair in a
true-lover's knot. The variety of these gifts is, of course,
endless, and it is, therefore, useless to say more on this head.
The fashion and your purse and good taste must dictate the
character of your gift in any case.

THE ENTERTAINMENT.

The entertainment at a silver wedding does not differ
materially from that at an ordinary reception. Sometimes
the pair stand under a marriage bell, as they did twenty-five
years before, and once more take the vows that bound them

for better or for worse. Following that they receive the congratulations of the guests, and then comes the cutting of the wedding cake, and the eager search for the ring. A bountiful feast, with toasts and speeches, crowns the celebration, which should be merry, and altogether hopeful.

THE CRYSTAL WEDDING.

The crystal wedding occurs on the fifteenth anniversary of the original marriage. It is not widely celebrated but many observe it with feasting and merry-making, the cards being in appropriate design, and the presents all of glass, in infinite variety.

THE TIN WEDDING.

On the tenth anniversary of marriage occurs the tin wedding, and this is the occasion of general jollity. The presents are all of tin, and the most surprising novelties are often provided for the occasion, including tin purses, tin fenders, tin chandeliers, tin fans, tin tables, and all imaginable things, useful and ornamental, within the range of the tinsmith's facile art.

THE WOODEN WEDDING.

Another gay celebration is that of the fifth anniversary, or the wooden wedding, when the cards are printed on beautiful bits of veneer, and the presents include everything in the range of wood-carving and cabinet-making. This celebration began as a joke within recent years, a step-ladder, a washboard, and a rolling-pin being the first gifts; but it has

now become an institution, and it is among the pleasantest
of the anniversary occasions.

THE CEREMONY, GIFTS, ETC.

Writing of anniversary weddings, a recent contributor to
the literature of the subject, declares that "the entertainment,
to be perfect, should occur exactly at the hour at which the
marriage took place, but as that has been found to be inconven-
ient, the marriage hour is ignored, and the party takes place
in the evening, generally, and with all the characteristics of a
modern reception. The bridal pair stand together, of course,
to receive, and as many of the original party of the groomsmen and bridesmaids as can be got together should be induced
to form a part of the group. There can be no objection to the
sending of flowers, and particular friends who wish, can, of
course, send other gifts, but there should be no *obligation*.
We may say here that the custom of giving bridal gifts has
become an outrageous abuse of a good idea. From being a
pretty custom, which had its basis in the excellent system of
our Dutch ancestors, who combined to help the young couple
by presents of bed and table linen, and necessary table
furniture and silver, it has now sometimes degenerated into a
form of ostentation, and is a great tax on the friends of
the bride. People in certain relations to the family are
even expected to send certain gifts. It has been known to
be the case that the bride allowed some officious friend to
suggest that she should have silver, or pearls, or diamonds,
and a rich old bachelor uncle is sure to be told what is

expected from him. But when a couple have reached their silver wedding, and are able and willing to celebrate it, it may be supposed that they are beyond the necessity of appealing to the generosity of their friends; therefore it is a good custom to have this phrase added to the silver-wedding invitations: "No presents received."

INTRODUCTIONS.

INTRODUCTIONS

Among certain barbarous peoples the exchange of names is the highest proof of amity, and in civilized society this idea survives in the formal introduction which etiquette demands whenever strangers are thrown together in social intercourse. In large cities people meet day after day for years in public conveyances, in stores and shops, on the street, or upon the stairs, without a sign of recognition, simply because the ceremony of introduction has never taken place. In the country the rule is less rigid, and intercourse between neighbors is seldom hampered by the conventionalities that are so great and perhaps so necessary a restraint in the great centers of social life. The resident of a village finds it hard to believe that his friend in the city should not know his next-door neighbor, whom he sees every day in the year; yet it is a fact that men living even under the same roof in Chicago or New York will grow gray together without ever once having exchanged so much as a nod, although each may know the other's name and be assured of his respectability; but nobody has ever said: "Mr. Brown, Mr. Smith; Mr. Smith, Mr. Brown;" and so Messrs. Smith and Brown remain as utterly strangers to each other as if the sea, and not the walls of a flat, divided them.

But this is established usage, and established usage is

stronger than law. It cannot be ignored with impunity, except in rare instances, as in the case of accident or calamity, when all rules yield to the emergency. We have read somewhere of an elderly spinister, a stickler for etiquette, who was about to be consumed in a burning house. A gallant stranger, perceiving her peril, at the risk of his own life, mounted the stairs, burst into her chamber and sought to carry her out. But she waved him off. "Go away," said she, faintly through the smoke, "I do not know you. We have never been introduced!" Perhaps the stranger would have been justified under the circumstances in leaving the lady to her fate; but he didn't. He broke down all conventionalities, seized the imperiled fair one in his stalwart arms and bore her through the smoke and flames in triumph, amid the plaudits of the crowd. But she never forgave him for his "rudeness" in presenting himself to her without an introduction.

Happily, however, this sort of folly is exceptional. A little accident on the rail will quickly bring all the passengers together, conventionalities being forgotten in the common danger and excitement. And so formalities are waived in times of distress and calamity. No one stands on ceremony where succor is needed. No one stops to study the proprieties when peril is nigh. It is only in the artificial surroundings of society, where there is peace and security, that barriers arise against possible intrusion and men defend themselves within conventional breastworks from their fellow-men. It is not for us here to moralize on this curious phase of social life, nor to question the justice and common sense of the usages which it has dictated and established. It is enough if we simply indicate these usages and leave the rest to the individual judgment of our readers.

BE SURE THE INTRODUCTION IS AGREEABLE.

One of the first things to be considered when you propose bringing strangers together is whether both will be pleased with the introduction. To introduce two people who do not want to know each other will not win for you the thanks of either; and therefore great prudence and caution should be exercised in all cases where there is the possibility of giving offense or occasioning embarrassment. And especial care should be taken where a lady is concerned. Where a man is introduced to an undesirable person it is comparatively easy for him to protect himself; but a lady cannot rid herself of an improper acquaintance with equal facility, and her reputation is much more likely to suffer from a doubtful association than a man. Hence it is very important that only those of unimpeachable integrity and unsullied fame should be introduced to her; and she owes it to herself to receive introductions only through such persons as she may rely upon with perfect confidence as to their judgment and prudence. If her father, mother, husband, brother or sister offer to introduce a friend, she may accept the new acquaintance without hesitation, as a rule, and so when near relatives and intimate friends make such an offer, she is justified in making no objection, although the latter are not to be relied upon so implicitly as the former.

HOST AND HOSTESS INTRODUCE.

The host and hostess at a ball introduce the guests to each other. This is a duty, but the guests may attend to this civility among themselves when there is occasion. But no one is to be presented to a lady without her express permission, which she must grant except in the case that she has some strong reason for refusing it.

INTRODUCTIONS AT BALLS.

At private balls abroad formal introductions are dispensed with, on the theory that only such people have been invited as are entirely worthy of respect, self-introductions being thus justified, the mere fact that the guests have been invited to meet each other offering a sufficient guaranty of all that is required. And this custom saves a great deal of trouble, but it is possible only in private houses. At a public ball partners must be formally introduced to each other by the master of ceremonies, but ladies are frequently careful to dance at such entertainments only with the members of their own particular parties or with gentlemen they have previously known.

FORMS OF INTRODUCTION.

Introductions are often bungled in a most distressing manner. The well-meaning person who undertakes the office becomes confused, forgets the names, or does or says some awkward thing that increases his embarrassment. This is generally due to inexperience, or to some doubt as to just how the ceremony should be performed; yet it is simple enough, in all conscience, and even the least experienced should be able to go through it without hesitation or embarrassment. When introducing two gentlemen, you should look first to the elder, or, if there is a difference in social standing, to the superior, and with a bow say to him, "Mr. Jones, permit me to introduce to you my friend, Mr. Smith;" then turn to Mr. Smith and say, "Mr. Smith, Mr. Jones." If either of the gentlemen has a title, do not fail to use it, as "Dr. Bill, allow me to introduce Gen. Cannon; Gen. Cannon, Dr. Bill." Where either gentleman has a peculiar distinction, it should be indicated in the introduction, as "Mr. Brown, I have the honor of introducing Mr. Thompson, author of 'The Death of a Hero.' Mr. Thompson, Mr. Brown, the painter." In introducing a gentleman to a lady, bow slightly to her and say, "Miss Romayne, allow me to introduce Mr. Montagu; Mr. Montagu (bowing to him), Miss Romayne." When several persons are introduced to one, the following form is perhaps the best: "Mr. Dane, permit me to introduce Mr. and Mrs. Frank, Miss Courtney, Mr. Barnard and Mr. Amber," bowing slightly to each when named. When the person introduced is a stranger in the city, it is well to mention his place of residence, thus: "Mr. Green, allow me to introduce Judge Orton, of San Francisco; Judge Orton, Mr. Green, editor of *The Dial*." Great care should be taken in pronouncing the names. To mumble them is to invite confusion and occasion embarrassment. By all means speak the names distinctly.

OFFERING THE HAND.

When gentlemen are introduced, it is customary, but not obligatory, for them to shake hands. They may do so or not, as they may elect. But an unmarried lady acknowledges the introduction of a gentleman by a bow only. Where two ladies are introduced, it is the custom, at least in country towns, for them to salute each other by kissing; but as it has been elsewhere remarked, it is a custom more honored in the breach than the observance. When young people are introduced to one older in years, and secure in social position, it is a graceful act on the part of the latter to extend his hand, and to speak a pleasant word or two by way of encouragement.

HONORING INTRODUCTIONS.

When persons have been formally introduced, they have certain definite obligations resting upon them which good breeding requires them to honor. They may not meet without recognition; they must treat each other civilly; and, if they do not desire the acquaintance to go beyond formality, the fact may be signified without rudeness, by a polite bow. This is modified in the case of ball-room introductions, it being optional with the lady whether she afterward recognize a gentleman with whom she may have danced. Nor does etiquette require that gentlemen who have met casually at the house, or in the rooms of a mutual friend, shall recognize each other afterward. They certainly may do so if they like, but if they choose to do otherwise, no social rule is broken.

WHEN INTRODUCTIONS ARE NOT OBLIGATORY.

Persons may or may not be introduced when they chance to meet at your house during a morning call. You need not introduce them if you do not choose to do so, or if you doubt whether the parties concerned would be gratified. Where it is known that an introduction would be agreeable on both sides, it may be given on such an occasion with perfect propriety. But where such introductions have taken place, it is optional with the parties concerned whether they recognize each other subsequently. They may continue, or drop the acquaintance, according to their pleasure, the decision resting, however, with the lady, if between lady and gentleman, with the married, or elder lady, if between lady and lady, and with the elder, if between gentlemen.

As it has been elsewhere stated, an introduction is not required when, in walking with one friend, you meet another. Indeed, an introduction should not be given unless there is some very good reason for it. Nor are itroductions required when friends, accompanied by strangers, meet in any public place. But sisters, brothers and relatives may always be presented to friends, even when casually met.

It is required of a gentleman that he shall raise his hat if introduced in the street to one of either sex.

ALWAYS INTRODUCE GUESTS.

But in the case of a friend who is visiting at your house it is required that every caller shall be introduced, and your callers must continue to recognize him as long as he remains your guest. So, also, introductions given at a party to a visiting stranger must be recognized as long as the visit continues. And when you meet a visitor at the house of a friend you are bound to show him every possible courtesy.

ADDITIONAL HINTS.

Informal introductions are permissible where travelers are thrown together, on shipboard, or in railway trains ; but much prudence should be exercised in this particular. An acquaintance thus begun ends with the journey. The advances of a fellow-passenger are to be repelled only where they are evidently dictated by improper motives, or are characterized by rudeness.

You are justified in resenting the introduction to you by a friend of one who is objectionable, and you may properly treat the act as you would any other insult.

If a friend introduces one of his relatives, you are bound to treat that relative with respect, and recognize him as an acquaintance, except where some very special reason exists to justify a contrary course

You are not required to introduce a friend with whom you may be walking, to another friend you may chance to meet on the street, even though the latter may stop for a minute's chat, or join you in your walk.

An introduction to one in authority upon whom you have called as a petitioner, cannot be presumed upon at any future time. It gives you no claim to acquaintanceship.

Letters of introduction should be given only where the

writer is entirely willing to stand sponsor for the person in question.   Especial caution should be exercised where a lady is concerned.

On the receipt of a letter of introduction you are required to treat the bearer with politeness, requesting him to be seated, and showing him any other small attention which the situation may demand, pending the perusal of the letter. When that has been read, you must then act promptly, not forgetting your friend, whose feelings and wishes you are bound to consider in what you do.   A lady should not present a letter of introduction to a gentleman in person, but enclose it to him with her card, leaving him to acknowledge its receipt by calling upon her.

STREET ETIQUETTE.

STREET ETIQUETTE.

It is often a very serious question with both ladies and gentlemen as to what is required of them by the rules of etiquette on the street. They may be reasonably versed in the proprieties of the ball-room and the parlor, and yet have only the haziest conception of the duties and civilities of the public thoroughfare. Whether a gentleman should recognize a lady first, or wait for her to recognize him; whether he may stop to speak with her; whether he should give her the inside or the outside of the pavement if he turn to walk with her; whether he should go first across a narrow crossing or let the lady precede him; whether he should offer his arm in a crowd; all these are serious questions that must at some time have perplexed most men; and there are other questions equally perplexing to ladies, which it is our present purpose to answer fully yet briefly in the following pages.

RECOGNIZING FRIENDS.

Gentlemen recognize their friends, if of their own sex, by simply lifting their hats; if of the opposite sex, they must not only lift the hat, but they must also bow. It is also proper for them to give this added mark of deference to clergymen, distinguished citizens and elderly men. In shaking hands with a friend a gentleman extends his right hand while lifting his hat with the left. The latter hand must never be extended. It is a breach of good manners to offer only a portion of the hand in performing this civil ceremonial.

In America the gentleman bows to every lady he knows, without waiting for her recognition, as he would do in England. It is her duty to acknowledge the civility with a pleasant smile and an inclination of the head. If the gentleman be smoking, he must remove his cigar from his mouth while bowing to the lady.

WHICH SIDE OF PAVEMENT TO TAKE.

When walking alone a gentleman must turn aside to a lady, to one carrying a load, to a clergyman, or to an old person. "The rule of the road" is varied only in these cases; the general law being to "keep to the right" in meeting and passing other pedestrians. This law applies to women as well as to men, and its strict observance will save a good deal of jostling and annoyance.

Ladies should always be given the inside of the pavement, even if the gentleman be obliged to change at every corner.

STOPPING ACQUAINTANCES ON STREET.

If a gentleman meet a lady who is walking with any one he does not know, he must not stop, nor must he stop if his companion is unacquainted with a lady whom he may chance to encounter. However, the lady has a perfect right to stop if she chooses. If she should stop, then the stranger must be introduced, and no member of the group is permitted to pass on and wait, whether the introduction is agreeable or not.

OFFERING ASSISTANCE.

It is not improper for a gentleman to offer assistance to a lady over a dangerous crossing, or in alighting from a carriage. She may accept such a courtesy without hesitating, and when it has been rendered the gentleman should raise his hat, bow, and pass on.

THE USE OF UMBRELLAS.

If a gentleman is walking with two ladies in a rainstorm, and there is but one umbrella, he should yield it to his fair companions, and walk outside. To do otherwise is absurd, for if he should walk between them he would bo perfectly protected himself, but the ladies would get the benefit of the innumerable little streams running off the umbrella.

NEVER STOP LADY ON STREET.

Gentlemen will not stop a lady on the street to converse with her, but will turn and walk by her side. If she should be accompanied by a male companion, it is well to be sure that your presence will not be an intrusion before venturing to join them in their walk.

OFFERING THE ARM.

A gentleman may offer his arm to a lady whenever her safety, comfort or convenience will be subserved, as in passing through a crowd, or over a slippery pavement. At night a gentleman always offers his arm to a lady companion, and also in ascending the steps of a public building. He should keep step with a lady with military precision, regulating his.

gait by hers.   To walk rapidly with a lady is not in good form, since it is generally a severe trial to her, and involves her in a good deal of awkwardness, and perhaps discomfort.

A gentleman walking with two ladies may offer an arm to each, but a lady may not thus sandwich herself between two gentlemen.

HOW TO CROSS A NARROW CROSSING.

In crossing a narrow walk, a plank or a slippery place, the lady may go first, the gentleman following close behind, to aid her if required.   If the distance is short, the gentle-man may step over and then give his hand to the lady.   If a gentleman meet a strange lady or an elderly gentleman at such a point, he may with perfect propriety offer his assist-ance.

ASCENDING AND DESCENDING STAIRS.

Gentlemen always precede ladies in going up-stairs, and follow them in coming down, unless, indeed, they walk beside them, in which case the arm is offered.

SMOKING IN PRESENCE OF LADIES.

The rule which absolutely forbids smoking in the pres-ence of ladies, even with their express permission, has lost its force to a very great degree, so that in these degenerate days gentlemen are even permitted to enjoy their cigars while walk-ing with their lady friends.   It is more polite, however, to avoid smoking under such circumstances.

It is an impropriety on the part of a lady to accept the offer of an umbrella from a strange gentleman.   Such an offer must be firmly, yet politely, declined. She may accept such a courtesy from an acquaintance, however, without a breach of good manners. In such a case the umbrella should be returned the moment she reaches her destination.

SHOPPING.

A cynic who was asked what was the chief end of woman said that it was "to go shopping." Of course this was unjust, but the fact remains that the business of shopping is one of very great concern to the fair sex, and in conducting it they have established, and most of them observe, certain rules which are designed to preserve the proprieties and to maintain the rights of others.

In the first place, it is held to be unladylike to enter a store unless you have a real errand. To go in "just to be going" is rude and necessarily annoying to proprietor and clerks.

It is a good idea to know what you want before you go into a store. To stand at a counter hesitating, or to be unable to tell the clerk what you came for, is a doubtful compliment to yourself. If you cannot come to a decision, retire from the store until your mind is made up. The time of the clerks is valuable.

If your purpose in visiting a store is not to purchase, but to examine goods for future selection, let the fact be known, and do not look at fifty things you do not want.

Do not ask for samples unless you mean to return for the goods. An apology for the trouble caused in such cases will be graceful. Always avoid giving unnecessary trouble.

It is considered ill-bred to lounge over a counter, or to put your elbows upon it. Thrusting aside other people is unpardonably rude. Stage asides and whisperings in a store are in very doubtful taste.

When your purchases have been made, order the bundles sent home. A lady loaded down like a packhorse is not the most graceful object in the world, and in a public conveyance she is little less than a nuisance.

If, while trading, you desire to chat with a friend, step aside for the time being, thus releasing the clerk. To keep him waiting while you exchange gossip is extremely inconsiderate. Nor should you call a clerk who is attending another customer. Wait till he is disengaged, and then make your wants known.

It is a serious rudeness to take hold of a piece of goods or an article that another is inspecting. If you want to examine it, await your turn. And in handling any article for sale be very careful that you do not soil or injure it in any way.

It is just as well to reserve your comments upon goods displayed. If you do not like them you do not have to buy, and sneering remarks about them may give offense, without helping matters in the least.

As it is rightly deemed impertinent to volunteer to a friend your opinion of a proposed purchase, so it is held to be equally impertinent to invite that friend's criticism of an article you think of buying, at least, while the friend is engaged. If your opinion is not invited, do not give it; and do not interrupt your friends to get the benefit of their judgment.

STREET ATTIRE.

Ladies of really good breeding will not go upon the streets, either on a shopping expedition or for other purposes, in flashy attire. On the contrary, they will dress soberly, if elegantly, and their deportment will be such as to attract the least notice. They will walk quietly, seeing and hearing nothing that they ought not to see and hear, recognizing acquaintances with a courteous bow, and friends with cordial, yet not effusive greetings.

FORM NO STREET ACQUAINTANCE

Whether young or old, they will form no acquaintances on the streets, and their conduct will be marked by a modest reserve, which will keep impertinence at a distance, and disarm criticism. The very appearance of evil must be avoided, and she is not a true lady who so carries herself in the public thoroughfare that loafers stare as she goes by, and "mashers" follow her with insulting attentions.

And this suggests the remark that gentlemen do not congregate at street corners, theatre doors, and on church steps for the purpose of staring at ladies as they pass. Cads do this, and loafers, but no self-respecting or respectable man is ever seen occupying a position which entitles him to the contempt of women, and to the righteous indignation of fathers, husbands and brothers.

LADIES ALONE AT NIGHT.

Ladies who venture out alone at night must not expect to escape notice, nor must they be surprised if they become the victims of rudeness and the subject of severe criticism. In country villages the rule is somewhat relaxed, it being a custom for two or more young ladies to go out for an evening walk, but even in these quieter communities it is better for ladies to go out after nightfall only when they can have the protection of male escorts.

ADDITIONAL NOTES.

It is in bad form to call out loudly to a passing acquaintance. Loud talking and laughing are alike reprehensible.

In walking with a lady, it is the province of a gentleman to carry her parasol, or any book or parcel she may have with her, and he should insist upon doing so.

Experience suggests the propriety of turning corners with a certain degree of caution. To go around at full speed is to run the risk of a collision, which may be both awkward and painful.

It is inadmissible to look back at one you have passed; only the vulgar do this.

A lady is not expected to recognize an acquaintance across the street.

A gentleman will return the salute of a stranger who may bow to the lady with whom he is walking. If he is walking with a gentleman friend who bows to a lady, he should also bow.

In shaking hands on the street, it is entirely unnecessary to remove the gloves.

RIDING AND DRIVING.

RIDING AND DRIVING.

In this connection the etiquette of riding and driving may very properly be considered. In earlier days horseback riding was almost universal, and our grandmothers and grandfathers were as accomplished in the saddle as our belles and beaux of to-day are in music and dancing. But riding is still a fashionable diversion and a healthful exercise, and at Newport and other resorts of the gay world of pleasure, a horseback dash across country is an exciting event, which divides attention with the dinner party and the ball. Some hints on the proprieties of equestrianism may be found useful.

"Keep to the right, as the law directs." This is the rule of the road, both for riding and driving.

GENTLE MOUNT.

In inviting a lady to ride, a gentleman must exercise great caution in regard to her mount. If he cannot offer the use of his own horses, or the lady does not designate an animal to which she has been accustomed, he must secure one of proved gentleness, and trained to the side-saddle and riding-habit. It is very dangerous to permit a lady to mount a horse which may be unused to a lady's hand or skirts; and the judgment of liverymen and grooms should not be trusted too far in so important a matter.

PUNCTUALITY.

Punctuality on the part of the gentleman in keeping an appointment to go riding with a lady is imperative. It can not be otherwise than disagreeable for her to sit in-doors, waiting, in her riding habit. Nor must she keep the gentleman waiting, for in that case the horses may become restive from long standing.

ASSISTING LADY TO MOUNT.

Before permitting the lady to mount, her escort must carefully examine the girths and stirrup of her saddle, and the bit and reins of the bridle. Not a strap or buckle should escape inspection, and every possible precaution should be taken against accident.

Having attended to this important preliminary, the lady must then be handed to her seat, her permission having first been obtained. If a groom be present, he should render no other assistance than that of holding the horse, standing at his head. The lady stands, with her skirts carefully gathered in her left hand, on the near, or left side, of the animal, her right hand on the pommel of the saddle, and her face toward the horse's head. The gentleman should face the lady, standing at the horse's shoulder. He should then stoop, so that her left foot may rest in his right hand. When she springs, the gentleman should, with a gentle firmness, lift her up, being careful, however, not to give her so great an impetus that she will overleap the saddle.

ON THE ROAD.

When she has safely got her seat, and you have placed her foot in the stirrup and smoothed out her habit, you may mount your own horse, and leave the lady to set the pace, keeping to the right, or on the off side, of her horse. When riding with two ladies, the gentleman should ride to the right of both if they are experienced equestriennes; but if they are inexperienced, he should ride between them, the better to afford them assistance should they require it; but a gentleman must never touch a lady's horse unless she actually needs his aid. Yet he must be very watchful, and ready for any emergency.

Whenever a gate is to be opened, an obstruction to be removed, or a doubtful or dangerous place to be crossed, the gentleman must ride ahead. He must pay all tolls, and when a fence or ditch is to be cleared he must leap first. He should also select the most desirable roads, and when there is a choice of sides, by reason of shade, or otherwise, he may ride upon her left, or drop behind her, thus allowing her to take advantage of it. As far as possible he must protect her from the dust and mud, and he must never ride at a faster pace than it may be agreeable for the lady to go.

ASSISTING LADY TO DISMOUNT.

In dismounting, a gentleman offers a lady his right hand, taking her left. His own left hand he uses as a step for her foot, declining it gently as soon as she rises from the saddle. A lady should not attempt to spring from the saddle. To do so is not only awkward, but dangerous.

When a gentleman on horseback meets a lady walking, he should dismount if he stops to speak with her.

THE SEAT OF HONOR.

In a carriage, where a coachman is outside, the seat of honor is that on the right hand, facing the horses. It is accorded the lady, an elderly person, or the guest. The seat facing the horses is always left to the ladies. If a lady and gentleman alone enter a carriage, the latter must occupy the seat facing her, unless she invite him to sit by her side.

HOW TO GET IN OR OUT OF CARRIAGE.

In entering a carriage one should be careful to have one's back to the seat to be occupied.

It is quite an art to enter or leave a carriage gracefully, and gentlemen cannot be too careful of what they do. To trample a lady's dress, or shut her shawl in the door is extremely awkward. In quitting a carriage the gentleman must get out first, even if he be obliged to trouble the ladies by stepping across in front of them. He must then assist them to alight, first taking care that their skirts shall not be soiled by contact with the wheels. Where there is a coachman present he may open the door of the carriage and let down the steps, but he must in no case be allowed to assist the ladies out. The gentleman himself must do this.

When the gentleman himself acts as driver, there are many little points of polite observance which he cannot afford to neglect. He must drive as close as possible to the mounting block, or curb, head his horse toward the middle of the road and back his vehicle slightly, and thus separate the fore and hind wheels in such a way that the lady may be helped in without damage to her apparel. If there is a hitching-post, it is well to tie the horse securely, so that you may be left perfectly free to assist the lady to her seat. Where you cannot tie the horse, you should keep a firm hold of the lines with one hand, while giving the other to the lady. When she has been seated you should carefully tuck her skirts in, and then you should take your seat, carefully adjusting the lap-robe before starting. She should be given as much room in the seat as possible, and you must be careful that your elbow does not jog her in the side by the motion of driving.

SETTING THE PACE.

The gentleman will adopt the pace most agreeable to his companion. If she is timid, he will not attempt to "show off." Ward McAllister relates an amusing anecdote in his "Society as I Have Found It," which very clearly illustrates the folly of "showing off" in this way. Mr. McAllister is telling of a picnic at "The Glen," a romantic nook near Newport. "A young friend of mine, then paying court to a brilliant young woman, came to me for advice," says the social autocrat. "He wanted to impress the object of his attentions, and proposed to do so by hiring two of the fastest trotting-horses in Rhode Island, and driving the young lady out behind them to the 'Glen' picnic. His argument was that it was more American than any of your tandem or four-in-hand, or postilion riding; that the pace he should go at would be terrific, and he would guarantee to do the seven miles in twenty minutes. He was what we call a thorough trotting-horse man; much in love; worshiped horses; disliked style in them, going in for speed alone. I tried to dissuade him.

" 'It will never do,' I said; 'it is not the fashion; the lady you drive out will be beautifully dressed, and you will cover her with dust; besides, the pace will alarm her.'

" 'Never fear that, my man,' he answered. The girl has grit; she will go through anything. She is none of your milk-and-water misses. I can't go too fast for her.'

" 'Have it as you will, then,' I said, and off he went to Providence to secure, through influence, these two wonderfully speedy trotters.

"We were all grouped beautifully at 'The Glen,' when, all of a sudden, we heard something descending the hill at a terrific pace. It was impossible to make out what it was, as it was completely hidden by a cloud of dust. Down it came with lightning speed, and when it got opposite to the major and me, we heard a loud 'Whoa, my boys; whoa!' and the vehicle came to a stop. The occupants, a man and woman, were so covered with mud and dust that you could hardly distinguish the one from the other. I ran up to the side of the wagon, saw a red, indignant face and an outstretched hand, imploring me to take her out. Seizing my arm, she sprang from the wagon, exclaiming: 'The horrid creature; I never wish to lay eyes on him again,' and then she burst into tears. Her whole light, exquisite dress was totally

On the Road.

ruined, and she a sight to behold. Turning to him I saw a glow of triumph in his face; his watch was in his hand. 'I did it, by Jove! I did it, and ten seconds to spare! They are tearers!'

"I quietly replied, 'They are, indeed, tearers; they have torn your business into shreds.'

" 'Fudge, man!' he said, 'she won't mind it. She was a bit scared, to be sure, but she hung on to my arm, and we came through all right.' He then sought his victim. I soon saw by his dejected manner, that she had given him the mitten, and as I passed him, slowly walking his horses home, I philosophized to this extent: 'Trotting horses and fashion do not combine.' "

Riding and driving are accomplishments in which it is desirable that all ladies and gentlemen should be proficient. To ride well, one must be taught early, and practice assiduously. Like athletics, riding cannot be learned from mere theoretical teaching. "A good rider, on a good horse," said Lord Herbert, "is as much above himself and others as the world can make him."

Ladies are not expected to exchange kisses in the king's highway, or in any other public place. That some women do this sort of thing is only another proof that good manners are too often neglected.

When a lady. wishes to leave a carriage temporarily, leaving the gentleman behind, he must alight to assist her out, and, when she returns, he must again get down to help her in.

WHO SHALL HOLD THE REINS?

When the owner of a wagon is driving a gentleman, it is courteous to offer the reins, but the offer should always be declined. In a long drive, however, the guest may offer to hold the reins for a time to rest the driver; but such an offer must not be made under any circumstances.

When one is driving, and meets a friend who is invited to a seat in the carriage, it is imperative that the guest shall be driven to his destination, no matter how far it may take the driver out of his way.

A gentleman must not put his arm across the back of the seat when driving with a lady. To do so is an extreme case of impertinent rudeness.

When offered a seat in the carriage of a gentleman friend, you should motion for him to be seated first; but, if he stands aside for you, bow and precede him.

TRAVELING.

TRAVELING.

In America, where everybody is something of a tourist, the etiquette of travel is not to be neglected. The boy on the farm to-day may be flying across the continent to-morrow for business or pleasure; and the girl whose little world is now bounded by the horizon of home, may yet see it expand, under the smiles of fortune, until it embraces that great outer region which exists for her to-day only in her waking dreams.

TRAVEL A GREAT CIVILIZER.

Travel is a great civilizer. Perhaps it is the greatest civilizer, unless Ruskin is right in claiming that honor for war, which itself involves travel, the exchange of ideas, as well as of bullets, the destruction of prejudice and insularity, as well as of forts and castles. Certainly it was the crusades that stimulated the great intellectual movement of the Western world. The rude warriors of England and France and Germany, in striving to rescue the Holy Sepulcher from the Paynim foe, gained not only glory, but knowledge. They acquired not only honorable scars, but a larger grasp of things. The civilization of Darkest Africa will follow the steamboat and the locomotive. Ignorance cannot long survive the influences of steam and steel rails. The man who travels is lost to the hosts of bigotry and narrow prejudice. He takes on the spirit of independence with the polish of social intercourse, and his mind broadens with the horizon of his enlarged experience.

The facilities of travel to-day are marvelous. The seven weeks' voyage across the ocean has been reduced to five days. Palace trains, on which the passenger sleeps, eats, takes his bath, is shaved, and enjoys every luxury of a first-class hotel, convey the tourist from New York to the Golden Gate at the rate of fifty miles an hour. The world is on wheels, and "All aboard!" is the cry that, soon or late, rings in every man's ears.

ILL BREEDING SHOWS ITSELF.

No situation can be named where the contrast between the well-bred and the ill-bred is sharper than in the railway carriage or the saloon of a steamer; and in the United States, where all classes are thrown together in the public conveyances, the annoyances of rude company are very trying. In England and on the Continent, there is greater exclusiveness, and the contrasts are less marked. But even in those countries, travel is not wholly free from the unpleasant features which Europeans so quickly note and so severely condemn in America.

BEING POLITE.

In the first place, selfishness is the besetting sin of the traveler. It shows in the rush for tickets, in the scramble for seats, and in the calm indifference to the comfort and convenience of others. Yet selfishness is no more to be defended when displayed on the railway train or in the steamer than if it were exhibited in the parlor or drawing-room. The rights of others must never be ignored; their convenience and comfort must never be sacrificed to your own.

Good nature, perfect courtesy, patience and an easy and affable adaptation to possibly untoward circumstances mark the lady and gentleman in traveling.

But it is generally through ignorance of polite usage, and not from native indifference to the rights and comforts of others, that many travelers make themselves disagreeable. They invite criticism and excite wrath simply because they have neglected to inform themselves upon the proprieties of the road. The observance of a few points of etiquette will at once save the travelers from the charge of boorishness, and tend greatly to the mitigation of the tedium and fatigue of a journey.

OFFERING AND ACCEPTING COURTESIES.

A lady traveling alone may, with perfect propriety, accept a courtesy from a strange gentleman, such as raising or lowering a window, the offer of a hand across a slippery gangplank, or any small attention; but she must be careful, in thanking him for his civility, to do so in a tone that will not encourage further advances.

On the other hand, a gentleman who is traveling alone may offer little courtesies to strangers, and even to ladies, carefully preserving a respectful manner, and avoiding the appearance of impertinence.

GENTLEMEN SMOKING.

They will not smoke in the presence of ladies, even if the rules of the railway, stage or steamer permit smoking.

In regard to smoking, it may be said, in a general way, that it should be studiously avoided in all places where it is likely to give offense. It is not enough to ask any lady who may be present for her permission to smoke. She will hardly refuse it, however disagreeable to her the smell of smoke may be. If only gentlemen are present, each individual must be consulted before your cigar is lighted. If any one of them objects, his voice should decide the day; for no gentleman has a right to insist upon his own gratification at the expense of another's comfort. Should no objection be offered, the gentleman who first strikes a light should offer it to others near him, before he uses it himself.

OPENING AND CLOSING WINDOWS.

A great deal of the annoyance and discomfort of railway travel is occasioned by the carelessness or indifference of some in regard to the windows. All the pleasure of a journey may be spoilt for half-a-dozen people by one person who may persist in having his window open, giving access to smoke and dust, as well as to fresh air. Here, again, the comfort of others must be first consulted. The person who sits facing the engine has the deciding voice as to whether the window shall be kept up or down; but ladies should always be consulted in the matter, whichever seat they may occupy.

WHEN A LADY MAY ACCEPT COURTESIES.

When a lady traveling alone wishes to descend from a railway coach, it is the duty of the gentleman nearest the door to assist her in alighting. He may offer to collect her baggage, call a hack, or peform any service which an escort might properly undertake.

If a train stop for refreshments, a gentleman may offer to escort a strange lady, who is alone, to the dining-room, or to fetch her anything she may desire. In case she accepts the offer, he must see that she is waited upon before attending to his own wants. A lady may always accept such an offer of attention, thanking the gentleman for his courtesy, and dismissing him with a polite bow, that he must accept as an intimation that his services are no longer required.

LADY WITH ESCORT.

When a lady has an escort, it is her duty to consult his comfort as well as her own. To weary him constantly by complaints; to worry over some unavoidable mishap or accident; to lose or misplace some of her hand baggage every few minutes; to tax his good nature about the time, the distance, and so on; to fidget about her baggage, or to quarrel with what he cannot control, is unladylike and reprehensible. Ladies, in traveling, are prone to do all these things, and thus their under-breeding shows itself. When one sees a lady, detained, perhaps, for hours by a snow-storm, pleasantly trying to beguile the time by conversation, relieving tired mothers of the care of fretful children, jesting lightly on the unpleasant delay, and uttering no complaint or impatient word, even if half frozen, or in utter discomfort, one may be quite certain of her breeding. But the escort must himself be punctilious.

TICKETS AND BAGGAGE.

He must carefully fulfill all the requirements of the rather arduous position he has the honor to hold. If the lady in question is to meet him at the wharf or railway station, he must be there a little in advance of the hour for departure, to procure her ticket, attend to her baggage and secure her a desirable seat. He must not leave her to stand in an office or upon a wharf while he is looking after her ticket and baggage. He must first seat her in the lady's room of the station, or in the cabin of the steamer, and then return for those duties. In arriving at a station, he must see her seated in a hack, or in the ladies' waiting-room, before he looks after the trunks.

AT THE HOTEL.

At the hotel he must escort the lady to the parlor before securing her room. He must then escort her thither, and, after ascertaining at what hour it will be agreeable to her to take the next meal, he must then immediately leave her. At the hour appointed for the meal the lady must meet her escort in the parlor. At the journey's end he must not leave her until he has seen her safely in the hands of her friends. If he remain in the city, he must call the next day to inquire after her health. After that the lady may continue the acquaintance or not, as she pleases.

A gentleman, on entering a public carriage or omnibus, must never step before a lady. He should stand aside for her, and must raise his hat slightly if she acknowledge his courtesy. If she appears to need assistance, he should offer it without hesitation, strangers though they be.

ADDITIONAL NOTES.

No lady should ever allow her escort, no matter what his relation to her may be, to enter any saloon or compartment devoted exclusively to ladies. This is imperative.

Under certain circumstances, a lady if married and not too young, may begin a conversation with a strange gentleman; but he must not, under any circumstances, begin a conversation with her. Unless she be well advanced in life, an unmarried lady is not supposed to begin conversation with a strange gentleman. On a long journey the rigid rules somewhat relax, and a certain degree of sociability may properly be indulged; but ladies cannot be too careful while traveling alone. They must maintain a quiet reserve, and, while graciously accepting and gracefully acknowledging every courtesy, must check every approach to familiarity.

SLEEPING CAR.

For traveling long distances, or where a night has to be passed on the cars, there is nothing that adds so much to one's comfort as the sleeping-car. Here you avoid all the noise and confusion caused by way passengers getting on or off. You enjoy an even temperature, which you cannot have in a day coach, where the doors are constantly being opened and closed. You secure a good night's rest. Then, too, your comforts are well looked after, which lessens the fatigue of the journey. Berths should be secured beforehand, when possible.

In the larger towns and cities this can be done by calling at
the ticket office. In smaller places the ticket agent will telegraph ahead and secure berths. Lower berths, located near
the center of the car, are most desirable. Ladies traveling
alone secure greater privacy by securing what is known as the
enclosed section. Failing in this, they should secure berths
near the end of the car where the ladies' dressing-room is
located. The conductor will always provide, so far as possible, for the comfort and convenience of his passengers, and
guard against any possible embarrassments.

The porter will arrange the berths to suit their convenience, as far as may be, and he should be applied to whenever any service is required. The conductor will supply all
needed information, and natural good taste and native modesty will guide them for the rest.

SECURING AND OCCUPYING SEAT.

A lady of good breeding will not monopolize more than
her rightful seat in a crowded car. When others are looking
for seats, she will immediately, and with all cheerfulness, so
dispose her baggage that the seat beside her will be at liberty
for any one desiring it. When the seats are turned together,
as they may be when the passengers are few, it is perfectly
proper for fresh comers to claim one of them, and the occu-
pant or occupants cannot reasonably object.

A gentleman may enter a car and secure his seat by de-
positing his coat or traveling-bag upon it, afterward going
out to get his ticket, or for any other purpose.

It is not required of a gentleman that he shall relinquish his seat in a railway car in favor of a lady, but gentlemen of good breeding will not retain their seats when a lady is standing. On a street-car it is different. The gentleman is bound by the rules of etiquette to resign his seat instantly if there is a lady standing.

ON BOARD STEAMER.

The same general rules that govern the conduct of ladies in a hotel should be observed on board a steamer. Her escort, if she have one, must meet her only in the ladies' cabin, or on deck. If alone, she must be circumspect in all her movements. Attendants will administer to all her reasonable wants, and the captain will supply any required information. Gentlemen will never fail to offer their seats on deck to ladies, unless there are vacant places.

BEING SOCIABLE.

The advances of fellow-passengers must be met half way. Over-exclusiveness is not a merit. It is too often mere boorishness, or positive rudeness. On a steamer the opportunities for social intercourse are greater than in a railway carriage, and these may generally be improved with advantage, and without impropriety, but here, as elsewhere, the lady must avoid the appearance of too great freedom of manner. The captain is a host who, in most cases, will attend to all the civilities of his position, and it need not be difficult to secure, through his offices, the social amenities necessary to break the monotony of a long voyage.

CONVERSATION.

Talking on a railway train to many people is very painful. To one with weak lungs it may be positively injurious, and it will be the part of good breeding to take this possibility into consideration when you may feel disposed to engage your traveling companion in conversation. A lady may with perfect propriety excuse herself from talking to her escort in case the effort to make herself heard above the din of the wheels is distressing.

TRAVELING ABROAD.

"In traveling abroad," says a recent writer, "the truest courtesy is to observe, as far as practicable, every national prejudice. The old proverb, to 'do in Rome as the Romans do,' is the best rule of etiquette in foreign travel. The man who affects a supercilious disdain of all foreign customs and forms, will not convince the natives of his vast superiority, but impress them with the belief that he is an ill-bred idiot. The most polite, as well as agreeable, travelers are those who will smilingly devour mouse pie and bird's-nest soup in China, dine contentedly on horse-steak in Paris, swallow their beef uncooked in Germany, maintain an unwinking gravity over the hottest curry in India, smoke their hookah gratefully in Turkey, mount an elephant in Ceylon, and, in short, conform gracefully to any native custom, however strange it may appear to them."

MAKING COMPARISONS.

" 'Comparisons are odious,' and to be continually asserting that everything in the United States is vastly superior to everything abroad is a mark of vulgarity. If you really think there is nothing to be seen abroad as good as you have at home, why, you are really foolish not to stay at home and enjoy the best."

PUBLIC PLACES.

PUBLIC PLACES.

Rude behavior in public places is never pardonable. There, if anywhere, gentle breeding will be revealed; and there, too, will sham gentility publish its true quality, either by boisterous and vulgar speech or by inconsiderate and selfish actions.

SUBDUED, RESERVED MANNER.

A subdued manner and a careful attention to the rights, convenience and comfort of others mark the well-trained man or woman wherever they may appear. They do not disturb an audience at the concert or play by loud whispering or ill-timed laughter; they do not scandalize the congregation at church by unseemly conduct; they do not stand in front of a picture in a gallery unmindful of the rights of other spectators; they do not rudely jostle in a crowd nor roughly jest at the expense of others' feelings. On the contrary, they are always thoughtful and courteous, always respectful in deportment and refined in manner, always on guard against the commission of any act that might distress or wound those about them.

THE CHURCH.

At church they will preserve the utmost silence and decorum.

They will display no haste in passing up and down the aisle.

They will not whisper, laugh, or stare about them.

The gentleman will remove his hat as soon as he enters, and will not replace it till he is again in the vestibule.

REACHING THE PEW.

He must pass up the aisle beside his lady companion until the pew is reached, then advance a few steps, open the door, and stand outside until she has entered. He will then follow her and close the door. He will not place his hat in the aisle. If there is not room for it on the seat, it can be placed on the floor inside the pew.

It is improper to bow to any friend while in the church itself. Greetings may be exchanged in the vestibule at the close of the services.

USE OF PEWS.

Persons visiting a church in which they have no pews of their own should wait in the vestibule till the sexton comes to show them to seats. It is highly improper to enter a pew uninvited or without permission. In most churches it is the custom to require strangers to wait standing until after the second singing, when it is permissible for them to occupy any seats that may be available. Pew holders coming in later must find seats wherever they can.

The holder of a pew, who may see a stranger enter a church, may silently invite him to a seat if there be room for his accommodation.

CONFORMING TO MODE OF WORSHIP.

Visitors to a church must conform strictly to the mode of worship. If the forms are unfamiliar, it is proper to rise, kneel and sit as the others do. Every ceremony and observance must be treated by the visitor with the utmost respect, no matter how grotesque it may appear to him. If he should find the services trying to his religious convictions, he need not attend a church of that denomination again; but he must not sneer at a form of worship while he is among those who practice it in as good faith as he practices his own.

A Protestant gentleman who attends a lady to a Roman Catholic church, may offer her the holy water, using his ungloved right hand.

Strangers should be provided with books. If the service is unfamiliar to them, the places for the day's reading should be indicated. It is perfectly proper to offer to share the prayer-book or hymnal with a stranger, if there are not separate books for his use.

In passing books or fans in church, the offer as well as the acceptance or refusal should be conveyed by a silent gesture.

NEVER GO LATE.

It is exceedingly ill-bred to go late to church. If you are invited to accompany friends to church, do not keep them waiting. If you invite them to accompany you, it is equally important that you should be ready promptly.

ADDITIONAL NOTES.

Ladies should not remove their gloves in church, unless to use the holy water, or in taking the communion. The right hand should then be ungloved.

It is very rude to begin the stir of preparation for leaving church before the services have been concluded. Put away your books, gather up your hat, wraps, etc., after the benediction; and do not push your way out.

Gentlemen will not congregate in the vestibule or on the church steps to stare at the ladies as they pass out. Only boors do this.

When visiting a church at home or abroad for the purpose of viewing the edifice or its adornments, choose an hour when there is no service. If you find even then that there are persons at their devotions, which is not unlikely, especially in the Catholic church, great care should be taken to avoid disturbing them. You should speak low, move softly, and preserve a respectful attitude, at the same time restraining any impulse of curiosity in regard to the worshipers.

PLACES OF AMUSEMENT.

On entering the hall, concert-room or theatre, the gentleman should walk side by side with his companion, unless the aisle is too narrow, when he should step a little in advance. Reaching the seats, he should hand her to the inner one, taking the outer one himself. In passing out, if he cannot offer his arm, he must again precede her until the lobby is reached. He will then offer his arm, and they will pass out, the gentleman taking care to protect his companion from rude jostling or from any crush.

DUTY OF ESCORT.

The gentleman must on no account leave the lady's side during the performance. If it be a promenade concert or opera, she may be invited to promenade during the intermission. If she decline, the gentleman must remain in his seat. To go out between the acts to smoke or for refreshments is an unpardonable breach of etiquette, and scarcely less than an insult to the lady. No gentleman will ever be guilty of conduct so reprehensible.

A gentleman is not required or expected to give up his seat to a lady. On the contrary, his duty is solely to his companion and he must remain at her side throughout the evening, to converse with her between the acts and to protect her in case of need.

It is perfectly proper to applaud, but boisterous demonstrations and loud laughter are not indulged by gentlemen. Applause should be given with the hands, and not with the feet.

It is the gentleman's duty to see that the lady is provided with a program. At the opera he should also provide a libretto.

COMPLETE QUIET SHOULD BE MAINTAINED.

Complete quiet should be maintained during the performance, that the audience may not be disturbed. It is in bad taste to distract your companion's attention from the stage, even if you find the performance dull yourself.   If you have occasion to speak to your companion while the curtain is up, do so in a low tone.   It is not in good taste to assume an air of mystery or secrecy in a public place; and lover-like acts should be studiously avoided.   To appear to comment aside on those near you is extremely ill-bred.

Ladies will not stare around the house through an opera glass.   It doesn't look well.   Extravagant gesture, loud laughter, a conspicuous use of the fan, all mark a lack of breeding in the lady.   And there is indecorum in a lounging attitude, in whispers aside and in toying with the opera-glass.

THE PROMENADE BETWEEN ACTS.

If you promenade at a concert or between the acts of a play, you may bow to friends the first time you pass them only.   A lady will not allow other gentlemen to join her if she would not offend her escort.   Gentlemen will not stop a lady to speak to her.   At such meetings only the briefest exchange of civilities is allowable.   A gentleman alone may join lady friends for a moment between the acts of a play or during the intermission at a concert; but he must not trench in the least upon the prior claims of their escort on their attention.

JOINING A THEATRE PARTY.

It is justly accounted a rudeness to join any party about to go to a place of amusement, unless urgently invited; and persons of taste will avoid the trying position of a third.   But if two or three ladies are in the party and but one gentleman, another gentleman, if his acquaintance warrants him, may offer his services as escort to one of the ladies. If he is not permitted to share the expenses, he should invite the party to join him in a little supper after the performance.

AFTER THEATRE CALLS.

It is courteous on the part of the gentleman to ask permission to call on the lady the day or evening following; and the lady should cordially grant it. She will make this call the occasion for intimating to him the pleasure he has afforded her, and she will avoid any criticism of the performance that may seem to reflect upon his judgment or taste in inviting her to witness it.

INVITING THE THIRD PARTY.

A gentleman who desires to invite a young lady to visit any place of public amusement with him, on the first occasion at least, must also invite another lady of the same family to accompany her. It is not considered good form for a young lady to go alone to a theatre, concert or opera with a gentleman with whom she is but slightly acquainted.

CHURCH FAIRS AND CHURCH BAZAARS.

Never make the blunder, when visiting a church fair or fancy bazaar, of criticising the articles displayed for sale. You cannot tell whose sensibilities will be wounded. Do not comment upon the display at all unless you can praise it. Do not mistake the fair for a cheap John store and try to cheapen the articles. Do not haggle over prices. Pay what is demanded, or do not buy.

A gentleman will remain uncovered while visiting a public place of this description, carrying his hat in his hand.

ASKING FOR CHANGE.

He may not ask for change in paying for an article; but it is rude for a lady to take advantage of this rule. Unless in presenting a bill representing a sum larger than the amount of the purchase he specifically request her to keep the remainder "for the good of the cause," the lady will return to him the exact change.

DEPORTMENT OF LADY.

"The position of a lady at the table of a fancy fair," says a recent writer, "is necessarily an exposed one, and requires a great amount of modest dignity to support it. Flirting, loud talking, importunate entreaties to unwilling friends to buy your goods, are all in bad taste; and it is equally bad to leave your table every few moments to visit the refreshment table with your gentlemen friends. We heard a lady boast once that she had been seventeen times in one day to the refreshment table 'for the good of the fair,' and we could not but think the cause might have been aided without quite such a display of gastronomic energy. No true lady will follow friends all around the room offering goods for sale, nor force articles on reluctant purchasers by appealing to their gallantry."

UNDER THE GREENWOOD TREE.

The picnic, especially in the smaller cities and the country towns, is the great event; and it is not despised, even in places like New York, Chicago, Philadelphia and San Francisco. It is affected by fashion at Newport, and the young men and maidens of rural villages look to it for their highest enjoyment; and perhaps no other form of social amusement is more inspiriting, more wholesome or more deliciously free from convention.

Yet the picnic has its etiquette as well as the ball and the dinner party; and society demands that under the greenwood tree, as under the chandelier, her rules shall be faithfully observed.

MUST BE PLENTY TO EAT.

First of all she demands that enough shall be provided for all to eat and drink. No one must be suffered to go home hungry; and as country air is a great sharpener of appetites, the amplest allowance must be made for every possible guest. Delicate young ladies who, at home, are scarcely equal to a thin slice of bread and butter, at the picnic will discover a capacity for cold chicken, deviled eggs, shrimp salad and other toothsome solids simply amazing; and pale young men who are doted on by their landladies because of their light eating will somehow manage to get through a picnic bill of fare, from the cold tongue to the cake and ice cream, in a way that would do credit to a farm-hand.

PROVIDING CONVEYANCES.

Conveyances are to be provided for all guests; and such conveyances should be covered, or capable of being covered, as a protection against the weather. The provisions should be forwarded to the picnic grounds in a separate wagon in charge of one or two servants; but these must not be permitted at dinner to interfere with the prescriptive picnic rights and privileges of the gentlemen of the party, who must officiate as waiters in ordinary to the fair guests of the occasion.

THE POPULAR PICNIC.

But the popular picnic is that in which a lot of people join for a day's outing. That is the sort of picnic the boys get up along in the leafy month of June or later in the sultry August days, and that is the event which takes the place of seaside vacation and mountain sojourn in the life of the average village belle.

In this sort of picnic somebody usually takes the lead, preparing a list of those to be invited. This list is generally submitted to one or two friends for scrutiny and approval, after which the persons included are severally notified of the proposed outing. Ordinarily the list embraces an equal number of ladies and gentlemen; and it is not unusual for each gentleman to be assigned to act as the escort of a particular lady. But this is not generally done except in cases where preferences are well known. The mismating of couples at a picnic is the worst thing that could possibly happen, and therefore no promoter of such an outing will undertake to

To the Picnic.

assign the ladies their escorts without a very careful consideration of fancies and predilections.

LADIES FURNISH THE DINNER.

The ladies are expected to furnish the dinner, which is usually substantial in character, and as varied as the taste and skill of the several purveyors may suggest. The gentlemen ordinarily provide the ice cream, ices and lemonade, the ladies supplying only such things as they may themselves cook or prepare.

GENTLEMEN MAKE ALL ARRANGEMENTS.

All the arrangements for the picnic grounds, the conveyances, etc., are made by the gentlemen. At the hour for starting, each gentleman calls at the house of the lady he is to escort, and there awaits the carriage, or other conveyance, taking charge of her basket and wraps. When the whole party is to go in one vehicle, it is the rule to call first at the house of the lady farthest away, picking her up with her escort, and then proceeding to gather up the others in the order of their distance from the point of final departure. At the picnic grounds the gentlemen attend to the water supply, and to getting the baskets and other things properly disposed, the ladies, at the appointed hour spreading the table, and then seating themselves, to be waited upon by their escorts, who must not fail in any possible attention or civility. It is quite the usual thing for the table to be spread in common, each lady contributing whatever she has brought. Her escort should not betray a fondness for the cookery of some fair one on the other side, or at the other end of the cloth.   But it were rude to refuse to partake of a dish offered by another lady.

AFTER-DINNER ENTERTAINMENT.

After dinner it is usual to pass the time in singing, or, if an orchestra be available, in dancing. This is varied by games of all kinds, croquet, tennis, cards, "blackman," " drop-the-handkerchief," blind man's buff, "tag," and the like, all time-honored, and delightfully ridiculous and merry. When tired of games and romping—for the rigidest disciplin- arian *will* romp a little when there is green grass under foot and a blue sky overhead, and a merry company all around— the party generally breaks up into little knots, and, perhaps, into pairs, and then who shall say what glances may be exchanged, what tender sighs may be breathed, what ardent words and soft responses may be spoken under the inspiration of such an hour and amid such scenes?

DUTY OF GENTLEMEN TO ENTERTAIN.

The duty of the gentlemen on such occasions, aside from the matters suggested, is obvious. They must do their best to be amusing and entertaining. If one gentleman have musical talent, let him play—the flute, cornet, violin, or what- ever it may be. If another can sing a good song, let him sing it. If another can tell a clever story, by all means let him not keep it back. Let each one strive to drive dull care away, and banish melancholy; but let no one forget that he is a gentleman, with ladies; let all remember that freedom and license are very different things.

GREAT LATITUDE IN DRESS.

It may be suggested finally, in this connection, that great latitude in dress is allowable for picnics. Ladies wear morning dresses and hats, and gentlemen attire themselves in light coats, wide-awake hats, caps or straw hats. A large bell, or gong, should be taken to call the party together, when required; and every member of the company should respond promptly. To fail in this were a discourtesy to the rest, and nothing can excuse such a breach of good manners.

THE ETIQUETTE OF BOATING.

There are certain customs and usages in connection with this interesting pastime that deserve to be noted and observed.

Gentlemen unaccustomed to the management of a boat should never venture out with ladies. To do so is foolhardy, if not criminal. Great care should be taken not to overload a boat. The frequent boating accidents that happen are in most instances due either to overloading, or to the inexperience of the man at the oars. Men who cannot swim should never take ladies upon the water.

ASSISTING LADIES TO THEIR SEATS.

When the gentlemen are going out with the ladies, one of them steps into the boat and helps the ladies in and seats them, the other handing them down from the bank or pier. When the ladies have comfortably disposed themselves, and not before, the boat may be shoved off. Great care must be taken not to splash the ladies, either in first dipping the oars or subsequently.

WHO SHOULD ROW.

If a friend is with you, he must be given the preference of seats. You must ask him to row " stroke," as that is the place of honor.

If you cannot row, do not pretend you can. Say right out that you can't, and thus settle it, consoling yourself with the pleasant reflection that your confession entitles you to a seat by the side of the ladies and relieves you from the possibility of drowning the whole party.

A POPULAR EXERCISE.

Rowing has become a great fad among the ladies in recent years, and it is to be commended as a wholesome and vigorous exercise. But it should be indulged only on quiet rivers or on private lakes. If ladies adventure into more frequented waters, they must at least have the protection of a gentleman. And in all cases they must wear costumes proper for the exercise, which requires freedom of movement in every part. Corsets and crinoline should be left at home, and a good pair of stout boots should complete an equipment in which a skirt barely touching the ground, a flannel shirt and a sailor hat are the leading features. Rowing gloves should protect the hands.

THE DRESS.

The ordinary rowing costume for gentlemen is white flannel trousers, white rowing jersey and a straw hat. Pea-jackets are worn when their owners are not absolutely employed in pulling the oar.

The Studio.

IN THE GALLERY AND STUDIO.

One or two broad general hints will suffice in regard to the etiquette of a picture gallery. The rules governing in other public places apply with equal force here. Gentlemen must enter the gallery unhatted, and remain so until they depart. Conversation must be conducted in a low tone; and whistling, loud laughter and other boisterous displays are not to be tolerated. In passing around to view the pictures, care should be taken not to pause long in one place, thus obstructing the view of others. When a gentleman is escorting a lady, he should provide her with a catalogue, and in passing through the picture rooms, he should offer his arm. It is his duty to protect her against jostling, and to find her a seat at intervals.

INVITATION NECESSARY.

The studio of an artist is not a public place, but it is one to which any member of the public may some time have occasion to go, and its etiquette is therefore important. In the first place, it is not to be visited as you would visit a photographer's or a picture dealer's. You must have received a special invitation or permission to make the visit; and when you go, it is not to be at your convenience, but at the time appointed by the artist.

PROPER DECORUM IN STUDIO.

Once there, you must keep your hand to yourself. To uncover any picture or article in a studio that may be veiled or hidden from view is the height of rudeness. It is not less rude to turn a picture that is hung or stands facing the wall; and the general rule of " hands off " applies to everything in the studio—pictures, busts, drapery, models, lay figures and what-not.

PRICING PAINTINGS.

It is a serious impropriety to ask an artist the price of his pictures on sight. "If a visitor sees a painting or a piece of statuary which he wishes to possess," says a writer on the subject, "he simply asks that he may have the refusal of it; or he says to the artist: 'I wish to have this picture, if it is not disposed of.' After leaving the studio, the visitor writes and asks the price, of which he is informed by the artist, in writing. Should the price be larger than the would-be purchaser is disposed to give, he writes again to that effect, and it is no breach of etiquette to name the sum which he wished to spend upon the work of art. This gives an opportunity to the artist of lowering his price. It is not customary, however, to haggle about the sum, and the correspondence should not be carried farther than above, except it be an intimation from the artist that he will accept the terms of the purchaser, and that the picture is subject to his order."

In the case of a portrait painter, the prices are usually designated in a scale conspicuously posted, half of which is usually to be paid after the first sitting, the remainder when the picture is delivered.

RUDE TO CRITICISE WORK OF AN ARTIST

It is unpardonable, rude and vulgar to criticise the artist's work in his presence. Fulsome praise is equally reprehensible. A few cordial words of compliment should certainly be spoken; and an intimate friend may venture to point out where improvements could be made. But the casual visitor must never assume the role of critic, and even the artist's intimates will do well to leave criticism to the public journals.

SITTING FOR A PORTRAIT.

If you are sitting for a portrait, do not keep the painter waiting. To do so is a serious matter, involving the loss of valuable time to him, and perhaps trenching upon the time of other clients. Nor should you detain him when the sitting is over. His urbanity may prevent him from hinting to you that you are trespassing upon his hours of work, though he may be silently fretting at your want of consideration in so doing.

Unless invited by the artist to do so, do not look around a studio in which you may be sitting. Do not ask to see an unfinished picture, even if it is one that is being painted by your own order.

ADDITIONAL HINTS.

Gentlemen must never smoke in a studio, unless invited to do so by the artist.

It is a breach of good manners to whisper in a studio.

It is rude and indelicate to behave in a studio as if you were in a store, pricing pictures, inquiring about what is for public exhibition, what is not; who ordered this picture or that; whose portrait this may be, and whose that; or in any way reminding the artist that his talent is mere merchandise.

Do not watch the artist while he is at work. Do not stand behind him or near him. He invited you to visit his studio, not to watch him work, but to view his pictures, and when you have done this, do not linger, but go.

A young child should not be taken to an artist's studio.

HOTELS.

HOTELS.

The modern caravansary is a world within four walls. It differs from the inn of olden times as the palace train differs from the stage coach, from which it has been evolved, and the life which ebbs and flows through its rotunda and corridors with the restless pulsations of feverish activity, is a reflex of that larger life that ebbs and flows without. Here come thoughtless pleasure and sated ambition. Here go youthful hope and old indifference. Yonder is the busy merchant side by side with the idle lounger, and over there the clergyman and the *blase* man of the world exchange civilities, while the cowboy from the plains and the great poet from the other side of the ocean, divide the curious attention of *habitues*. In the parlor a wedding is in progress, while in a suite of rooms above, a scene of death is being enacted. A gay party of young men, in one of the apartments, are singing a bacchanal song that curiously discords with the lullaby of a mother in the next. Birth and death, joy and misery, pleasure and business, lofty ambition and listless indifference, high breeding and no breeding, pompous wealth and shrinking poverty— all the contrasts of the big world without, are here epitomized. And here, as elsewhere, the proprieties of life must be observed.

IGNORANCE BETRAYS AT ONCE.

A boor may remain undetected and unsuspected at

home, but how soon the truth appears after he has registered himself at a great hotel! How soon his ignorance and selfishness betray him, and how quickly the line is drawn between him and his fellow guests! The servants instantly recognize his lack of breeding, and secretly despise, even if they do not openly scorn, him. He is shunned in the lobby and avoided at table, and he does well indeed if he receives as good attention as others who pay no more for their entertainment.

No one need invite the resentment of guests and the ridicule of servants in a hotel. Attention to the usages of good society in this respect, as in others, is a prime requirement, and even the dullest may save himself from singularity by observing those simple rules of etiquette which good taste and common sense have suggested.

ADVICE TO GENTLEMEN.

Most of these have been detailed under other heads, and as far as gentlemen are concerned, only a very few words in this connection are required. They must curb their selfishness in a hotel as they would curb it in the house of a friend. The rights of others must never be ignored. A quiet demeanor is a first requisite. Loud talking, whistling, singing and boisterous laughter are intolerable. Staring across the diningroom at other guests, or being obtrusively curious in observing their movements, cannot be excused. At table the ordinary usages of good society govern. The napkin is not to be used as a bib; the knife must not be employed as a shovel; the

finger-bowl must not be mistaken for a goblet, and it is well to
avoid those dishes which are unfamiliar, and in the eating of
which it may be a matter of uncertainty whether a spoon or
a fork will be required.

ADVICE TO LADIES.

For ladies, the etiquette of hotel life may be given in
greater detail. In this country, where women so often travel
without escort, the following hints for their guidance will prove
invaluable. If duly observed, they will save much embarrassment, and perhaps preserve the fair traveler from annoyance
and insult.

ARRIVING AT HOTEL.

In arriving at a hotel a lady should go to the ladies'
entrance. She should never pass in or out through the public entrance, not even with an escort.

When a lady arrives at a hotel, she should send at once
for the proprietor. If she is provided with a letter of introduction to him, so much the better. Otherwise she will present her card, and mention the time for which she desires to
secure an apartment. She will not enter the public office,
but will go at once to the ladies' parlor, whence she will send
to the proprietor or clerk, and await there her assignment to
a room.

GO AND COME QUIETLY.

In passing to and from her apartment, she should not
stand or linger in the halls. To do so is to invite rudeness.
She must go and come quietly, and she will consult good taste
by dressing in the least conspicuous manner.

RECOGNIZING FRIENDS.

A lady is not expected to recognize her friends across the parlor or dining-room of a hotel. Greetings offered by other ladies at the table or in the parlor, should not be too hastily checked, as the acquaintance so formed is not required by etiquette to be recognized elsewhere.

AT MEALS.

In going to meals one of the waiters should meet her at the dining-room door and escort her to the table, saving her the awkwardness of crossing the floor alone, and showing other guests that she is a regular resident of the house. She may retain the services of this waiter during her stay, and it will be proper for her to give him a suitable present of money before departing.

She should not go alone to the supper-table after ten o'clock. If she return from an entertainment at a later hour, and has no escort to supper, she should have the meal sent to her room.

In giving an order at a public table, a lady should decide quickly what dishes she desires. The order should be given in a low, distinct tone. She must not point to any dish she wants passed to her. If she cannot name it, a well-trained waiter will understand her wishes if she simply looks at the dish.

It is exceedingly " bad form " to stare around the room, fidget with the napkin, or play with the knife, fork or spoon. It is allowable to look over a newspaper at breakfast, while your order is being filled, but it is scarcely permissible to carry a novel to the table.

If a lady accepts any small civility from a gentleman at the same table, such as handing the sugar, she must thank him, but she must not permit the opening of a conversation.

If a lady have friends at the table, conversation in a low, quiet tone is entirely proper; but any loud talk or laughter, or any extravagant gesticulation, is forbidden by the rules of good taste. It is exceedingly ill-bred to comment upon others present, either aloud or in a whisper. Any bold action or boisterous conduct in a hotel will expose a lady to the most severe censure, and possibly to misconstruction and impertinence.

IN THE PARLOR.

No lady should open a window in a hotel parlor if there are other ladies near it, without first consulting them. Nor should she use the piano of a hotel uninvited, if there are others in the room. It looks bold and forward to display even the most finished musical training in this way; and singing is still worse.

It is not permissible for a lady to stand alone at the front windows of a hotel, or walk out on the porch, or in any other conspicuous place. She must not loll or lounge in a public parlor, and papers, books or music found in that apartment must never be carried to your own room.

ADDITIONAL NOTES.

Jewelry and money should be deposited with the clerk, to

be rung for when wanted.   Trunks and hand-bags should be carefully locked whenever you go out.

A lady must never go herself to the door of a hotel to call a conveyance.   Ring for the servant to perform this office, and he will have the carriage brought to the ladies' entrance.

It is not allowable to scold the servants.   If they are negligent or disrespectful, complain to the housekeeper or the landlord.

Baggage should not be touched by a lady after it has been packed for her departure.   The servants will attend to its removal, and they should carry to the hack even the traveling shawl, satchel and railway novel.   It is not a pleasing spectacle to see a lady stumbling up the steps of a hotel hack.

THE TABLE.

THE TABLE.

The etiquette of the table is of the first importance. Its neglect at home is a most serious matter, and the parents who fail to impress upon their children at every meal the duty of observing the courtesies and decent usages of the table commit a fault that cannot be too sharply reprehended. A writer has justly observed that it is impossible for a lady or gentleman to act with ease and grace at table when in company, at a hotel or any public place, unless they habitually pay attention to those minor points of etiquette, which form so distinctive a mark of good breeding. Habitual neglect of these details of table courtesy and usage will make them appear awkward restraints upon occasions when they are important. Children should be taught at home to be polite and attentive at the table, and the parents who see to this need have no fear that their offspring will shame them when away from home by rude manners and awkwardness. Even one who eats alone ought to observe the rules of politeness. To do otherwise is to run the risk of forming awkward habits that he will not easily shake off in company.

The following anecdote from the French is appropriate: The poet Delille and Marmontel were dining together one April day in 1786, when the conversation chanced to turn on dinner table customs. Marmontel observed how many little things a well-bred man was obliged to know if he would escape being ridiculous at the table of his friends.

"They are, indeed, innumerable," said Delille; "and the most annoying fact of all is, that not all the wit and good sense in the world can help one to divine them untaught. A little while ago, for instance, the Abbe Cosson, who is professor of Literature at the College Mazarin, was describing to me a great dinner to which he had been invited at Versailles, and to which he had sat down in the company of peers, princes and marshals of France.

" 'I'll wager, now,' said I, 'that you committed a hundred blunders in the etiquette of the table.'

" 'How so?' replied the Abbe, somewhat nettled. 'What blunders could I make? It seems to me that I did precisely as others did.'

" 'And I, on the contrary, would stake my life that you did nothing as others did. But let us begin at the beginning, and see which is right. In the first place, there was your table-napkin—what did you do with that when you sat down at table?'

" 'What did I do with my table-napkin? Why, I did like the rest of the guests; I shook it out of the folds, spread it before me, and fastened one corner to my button-hole.'

" 'Very well, *mon cher*, you were the only person who did so. No one shakes, spreads and fastens a table-napkin in that manner. You should have only laid it across your knees. What soup had you?'

" 'Turtle.'

"'And how did you eat it?'

"'Like every one else, I suppose, I took my spoon in one hand and my fork in the other.'

"'Your fork! Good heavens! None but a savage eats soup with a fork. But go on. What did you take next?'

"'A boiled egg.'

"'Good; and what did you do with the shell?'

"'Not eat it, certainly. I left it, of course, in the egg-cup.'

"'Without breaking it through with your spoon?'

"'Without breaking it?'

"'Then, my dear fellow, permit me to tell you that no one eats an egg without breaking the shell and leaving the spoon standing in it. And after your egg?'

"'I asked for some *bouille*.'

"'For *bouille!* It is a term that no one uses. You should have asked for beef—never for *bouille*. Well, and after the *bouille?*'

"'I asked the Abbe de Baden-villais for some fowl.'

"'Wretched man! Fowl, indeed! You should have asked for chicken or capon. The word "fowl" is never heard out of the kitchen. But all this applies only to what you ate; tell me something of what you drank, and how you asked for it?'

"'I asked for champagne and bordeaux from those who had the bottles before them.'

"'Know, then, my good friend, that only a waiter who has no time or breath to spare, asks for champagne or bor-

13

deaux. A gentleman asks for vin de Champagne and vin de Bordeaux. And now inform me how you ate your bread.'

" 'Undoubtedly like all the rest of the world. I cut it up into small pieces with my knife.'

" 'Then, let me tell you that no one cuts bread; you should always break it. Let us go on to the coffee. How did you drink yours?'

" 'Pshaw! At least I could make no mistake in that. It was boiling hot; so I poured it, a little at a time, into the saucer, and drank it as it cooled.'

" '*Eh bien!* then you surely acted as no other gentleman in the room. Nothing can be more vulgar than to pour tea or coffee into a saucer. You should have waited till it cooled, and then have drank it from the cup. And now you see, my dear cousin, that so far from doing precisely as the others did, you acted in no one respect according to the laws prescribed by etiquette.' "

The story is a good one, and its moral plain. It shows that even a learned professor may grievously blunder in his table manners, and suggests the wisdom of making one's self familiar with the rules that polite society has established in this regard. A few hints here will be found useful.

GENERAL HINTS.

Sit neither very near nor very far from the table. Ladies, after seating themselves, should so dispose their skirts that others will not be crowded.

Never open the napkin entirely. Let it lie on tho lap, partly folded.

A gentleman will always see that ladies are served before he begins to eat.

Avoid making any noise on your plate with knife and fork.

Low breeding is distinctly marked by smacking the lips, by sucking the soup with a gurgling sound, by chewing meat noisily, by swallowing as with an effort, and by breathing heavily while masticating the food.

It is not less ill-bred to put large pieces of food into the mouth. If you should be addressed suddenly while your mouth was so filled, you would either have to make a very awkward pause before speaking, or else run the risk of strangulation by attempting to swallow the mouthful too hastily.

It is rude to move your arms at table in such a way as to incommode your neighbors, and to lean back in the chair, or to tilt it, is quite unpardonable. You are required to sit erect, not stiffly, but in an easy position.

It is decidedly inelegant to eat rapidly, and to eat very slowly is an affectation. It is well to preserve a happy medium.

Bread must never be cut, nor bitten. It is to be always broken; and to use it for soaking up gravy is inexpressibly vulgar. It is equally vulgar to scrape up sauce with a spoon, and to take up bones with the fingers.

Accustom yourself to eat with the left hand, thus avoiding the necessity of shifting the fork from one hand to the other. Never hold your knife and fork erect in your hands at each side of your plate, and do not cross them on your plate till you have finished eating.

When a plate has been sent to you filled with the food you have selected, keep it, as others may not have the same choice. If the plate contain one dish, such as pie or pudding, you may pass it on to those beside you, and wait till others above you are served before reserving a plate for yourself. Do not ask for a second helping. It is the duty of those at the head and foot of the table to offer that.

As you will not pour your coffee or tea into the saucer to cool it, neither will you blow your soup. Give the coffee and the soup time to cool, and then proceed to enjoy them.

In passing your plate to be served, or your cup to be refilled, remove the knife and fork, or the spoon, the latter to be placed in the saucer, and the former on the table. The salt-spoon, butter-knife and sugar-tongs should always be used.

In the event that you want to cough or sneeze, leave the table, if possible. If not, lean back and turn your head. A sneeze, it is said, may be suppressed, by placing the finger firmly upon the upper lip.

Don't use the table-cloth for a napkin. Don't pick your teeth with a fork. Don't put your fingers in your plate. And don't wipe your face with your napkin.

When dining out, the napkin is not folded up, but placed beside your plate when the meal is over. At home, where a napkin-ring is used, it is proper to fold the napkin up and place it in the ring when you are done with it.

It is unutteraby rude to find fault with the food, and it is no longer in good form to decline taking the last piece on a plate. That is an old-fashioned bit of propriety which is now more honored in the breach than in the observance.

It is improper to hurry away from the table as soon as you finish eating, if others remain to converse. In the event that you are called away before the conclusion, ask to be excused for leaving, and express your regrets for the necessity of so doing.

These rules and suggestions are general, and they apply at home and in company; no one can afford to slight them; and no one who is thoroughly familiar with them need fear that he will make a spectacle of himself when he is thrown among polite society.

Conversation graces meat, but no subject should be broached at table that is likely to excite disgust. Only the most refined topics should be introduced, and care should be exercised that no allusion is made or hint given that could offend the delicate sensibilities of guests who, without affectation, may be exceedingly sensitive on such points. A good meal may be wholly spoiled for some by the suggestion of a disgusting object or association.

A hair in the soup, a fly in the butter, a worm in the fruit, should be removed quietly. To do otherwise is unpardonable. If a fly falls into your coffee, do not mention the fact, but silently send your cup away to be refilled.

All small preferences for different wines or dishes should be kept in the background. Dishes and wines should not be mentioned unless they are on the table.

Anything like greediness or indecision is ill-bred. The

choicest pieces are ignored; and you must not take up one piece and lay it down in favor of another, or hesitate whether you will partake of the dish at all.

Where silver fish-knives are not found on the table, a piece of crust should be taken in the left hand, and the fork in the right, thus avoiding awkwardness in eating the fish.

BEGIN TO EAT AS SOON AS HELPED.

As soon as you are helped at table, begin to eat. It is old-fashioned and ill-bred to wait for others. If the food is too hot to begin eating of it at once, take up the knife and fork and appear to begin.

KNIFE, FORK AND SPOON.

Do not abuse knife, fork or spoon. Perhaps it is unnecessary to suggest that the knife must never be carried to the mouth. Cheese must be eaten with a fork, as likewise peas and most vegetables. Only puddings of a very soft kind and liquids require a spoon. In eating soup, always remember to take it from the side of the spoon.

Neither soup nor fish should be taken a second time. Whenever there is a servant to help you, never help yourself. When he is near catch his eye and ask for what you want. To drink a whole glassful at once or drain a glass to the last drop is ineffably vulgar.

Mustard, salt, etc., should be put at the side of the plate; and one vegetable should never be heaped on top of the other. In eating, one should not bend the head voraciously over the plate. The plate must never be tilted on any occasion. The wine-glass is to be held by the stem, and not by the bowl.

EATING ASPARAGUS.

In eating asparagus, there appears to be no settled rule. It is well, therefore, to observe what others do, and act accordingly. The best plan, perhaps, is to break off the heads with the fork, and thus convey them to the mouth. In France everybody takes up the asparagus with the fingers.

EATING CHERRIES, PLUMS, ETC.

In eating cherries, plums, etc., the same diversity of fashion prevails. Some put the stones out of the mouth into the spoon, and so convey them to the plate. Others cover the lips with the hand, drop the stones unseen into the palm, and so deposit them on the side of the plate. Very dainty feeders press out the stones with a fork in the first instance, and thus avoid the difficulty. This is recommended as the safest way for ladies. Fruit is eaten with a silver knife and fork.

FINGER-BOWLS.

Finger glasses, containing water slightly warmed and perfumed, are placed to each person at dessert. Into these you dip your fingers, wiping them afterwards on your table napkin.

CONVERSATION.

It is not well to talk too much at dinner. Very few have the genius to eat and talk well at the same time. One must observe the golden mean between dullness and brilliancy, remembering that a dinner is not a *conversazione*. In talking at table, gesticulations are objectionable. Nothing can well be more awkward and disconcerting than to overturn a wineglass, or upset the sauce upon the dress of your nearest neighbor.

DINNERS.

DINNERS.

It were not easy—nay, it is not possible—to over-estimate the importance of dinners. Ward McAllister, the autocrat of the drawing-rooms and a prince among entertainers, won his premiership of the Four Hundred by his mastery of the art of good feeding. "Providence," said the illustrious Dr. Prout, "has gifted man with reason; to his reason, therefore, is left the choice of his food and drink, and not to instinct, as among the lower animals. It thus becomes his duty to apply his reason to the regulation of his diet; to shun excess in quantity, and what is obnoxious in quality; to adhere, in short, to the simple and the natural, among which the bounty of his Maker has afforded him an ample selection; and beyond which, if he deviates, sooner or later he will pay the penalty."

It is said, with no little justice, that every man, the wise as well as the foolish, is a slave to his cook. And fortunes are made and marred by the influences of digestion, as witness the story related of Napoleon who is said to have lost two great battles—those of Leipsic and Borodino—because he had dined in great haste! And was not there once a great king who died of an over-gorge of lampreys, thus changing the course of history? What a warning! And we doubt not that history could supply thousands of instances in which an abused digestion has wreaked no less important revenges.

"The life of man," says the renowned Dr. Lancaster, " is like a fire. Just as the fire must have fuel in order that it may burn, so we must have food in order that we may live," and the analogy is in many respects quite correct, for we find that man really produces in his body a certain amount of heat, just as the fire does; and the result of the combustion of the materials of his food is the same as the result of burning fuel in a fire. Man exists, in fact, in consequence of the physical and chemical changes that go on in his body as the result of taking food." And further on he says: "Cooks in the kitchen, and ladies who superintend cooks and order dinners for large families, never think of asking whether food contains the right proportions of those ingredients which secure health; yet, without these, babies get rickets, young ladies acquire crooked spines, fathers get gouty, mothers have palpitations; and they do not think of ascribing these things to the food, which has deprived them of the proper constituents of their food."

But it is not our purpose to discuss the scientific phases of the food question. We merely wish to impress upon the minds of our readers the importance of good cookery, and to urge upon every housewife the duty of obtaining the best possible dinners for her family that her means will afford. Indifference to food is not a heroic virtue, and she should not permit a false sentiment to obscure the fact. Man is what he eats and woman is the caterer. If she perform her duty well her reward in domestic tranquility and inward peace will be ample.

DINNER-GIVING.

In another chapter the etiquette of the table has been detailed. In this chapter the subject of dinner-giving will be considered, and light from the best sources will be thrown upon it. Ward McAllister, for example, in his chapter on "Entertaining," in "Society as I Have Found It," says that "the first object to be arrived at is to make your dinners so charming and agreeable that invitations to them are eagerly sought for, and to let all feel that it is a great privilege to dine at your house, where they are sure to meet only those they will wish to meet. You cannot instruct people by a book how to entertain," he continues, "though Aristotle is said to have applied *his* talents to a compilation of a code of laws for the table. Success in entertaining is accomplished by magnetism and tact, which, combined, constitute social genius. It is the ladder to social success. If successfully done, it naturally excites jealousy. I have known a family who for years outdid every one in giving exquisite dinners—driven to Europe and passing the rest of their days there, on finding a neighbor outdoing them. I, myself," the leader of the Four Hundred goes on, "once lost a charming friend by giving a better soup than he did. His wife rushed home from my house, and in despair, throwing up her hands to her husband, exclaimed, 'Oh! what a soup!' I related this to my cousin, the distinguished *gourmet*, who laughingly said: 'Why did you not at once invite them to pork and beans?'"

In planning a dinner, the question is not to whom you owe dinners, but who is most desirable. The success of the dinner depends as much upon the company as the cook. Discordant elements—people invited alphabetically, or to pay off debts—are fatal. The next step is an interview with your *chef* or *cordon bleu*, whom you must arouse to fever heat by working on his ambition and vanity. You must impress upon him that this particular dinner will give him fame and lead to fortune. This accomplished, the question of soups and fish and entrees and dessert must be settled, and this safely done, nothing remains but to await the event.

THE NUMBER OF GUESTS.

The number of guests at a dinner party depends on the size of the room and the size of the table. Brillat Savarin, the great French authority, laid down the rules that the numbers at a dinner party should not be less than the Graces nor more than the Muses, and this rule is justly esteemed a good one. Even numbers, however, are to be desired, as more convenient, and the number of ladies and gentlemen should be equal.

SEATING GUESTS.

In this country questions of precedence are not strictly observed as in England, but even here the more distinguished guests are accorded the places of honor. When the parties are assembled—and it is imperative that every invited guest shall be punctual to the minute, neither late nor too early—the mistress of the house will point out to each gentleman the lady whom he is to conduct to table. The Boston fashion of one's finding, on entering the house in which

he was to dine, a small envelope on a silver salver, in which
was inclosed a card bearing on it the name of the lady assigned to him to take in to dinner, though still in use in New
York, is gradually dying out. Yet it has its obvious advantages. Great discretion and tact are required in making
these assignments. A judicious host or hostess will consider
the politics, religious opinions and tastes of the guests.
Quicksands will thus be avoided and the party will more certainly prove a social success.

"In going in to dinner," says a leading authority, "there
is but one rule to be observed. The lady of the house, in
almost every case, goes in last, all her guests preceding her
with this exception, that if the president of the United States
dines with you, or royalty, he takes in the lady of the house,
preceding all the guests. When no ladies are present, the
host should ask the most distinguished guest, or the person
to whom the dinner is given, to lead the way in to dinner,
and he should follow all the guests. The cards in the plates
indicate his place to each one. By gesture alone, the host
directs his guests to the dining-room, saying aloud to the
most distinguished guest, 'Will you kindly take the seat on
my right?'"

CONVERSATION.

Tact must be exercised in the distribution of your guests
at dinner. If among them there is a wit, or a clever talker,
he should be placed near the center, where he can be heard and
talked with by all the rest. If there be two such, do not seat
them near each other, for in that case they will extinguish

each other. Nor should two gentlemen of the same profession be placed side by side. They will probably fall to talking "shop" and thus cease to be entertaining except to themselves. A New York social star says, "that at table conversation should be crisp; it is bad taste to absorb it all. Macaulay, at a dinner, would so monopolize the conversation that Sydney Smith, the great wit, said that the historian did not distinguish between monologue and dialogue."

YOUNG GUESTS SPOIL A DINNER PARTY.

It is the dictum of good society that very young ladies and gentlemen should not be invited to dinner parties. "Young people," says the clever author of "Miss Majoribanks," "are the ruin of society." They are certainly the ruin of dinner parties.

DISHES NOT PLACED ON THE TABLE.

The fashion of dinners has been revolutionized since our grandfathers' days. Indeed, the changes within very recent years have been very marked. Dishes are now never placed on the table at a dinner of ceremony, and rarely even at small friendly dinners; and few people will resort to the old mode who have once tried the new.

THE TABLE.

An important point is the shape of the table, the circular and oval forms being preferred as offering superior advantages for conversation. The horse-shoe table is adapted to state banquets only; and the old-fashioned parallelogram is no longer in favor.   At the oval table the host and hostess face each other on opposite sides.   According to the French custom the host and hostess sit side by side at the middle of the table.

THE DINING-ROOM.

It is decreed by fashion and by common sense as well that, even in the heat of summer, the dining-room must be carpeted.   Otherwise the shuffling of feet will be annoying. Chairs with slanting backs are deemed the most desirable. The temperature of the room should be about 68 deg. Fahr. The presence of flowers on the table is in the best possible taste, and a small glass vase containing a *boutonniere* at every cover is very dainty, the guests removing the bouquets on leaving the table.   At the best New York houses, however, the corsage and button-hole bouquets are no longer seen.   In the matter of light it is well to be conservative.   A lamp on the table is not to be commended, and gas by many is deemed intolerable.   A careful arrangement of wax candles is preferable to any other mode of lighting.   The candles should be of real wax and not less than two to the pound.   Written bills of fare are laid to every two guests.

THE SERVANTS.

The servants should be well-trained, silent, observant, carefully dressed and scrupulously clean.   One servant to every two guests, or at least one to every three, is required. However, if only two servants are in attendance, one should begin with the guest on the host's right, ending with the lady of the house; the other with the guest on the hostess' right, ending with the master.

GRACE.

If clergymen be present, the one highest in rank is asked to say grace, except where the master of the house is a churchman, when he himself pronounces the ceremony.

PROLONGED WINE-DRINKING CONDEMNED.

At dinner parties ladies seldom eat cheese, drink liquors, or take wine at dessert. Coffee, after the excellent foreign custom, is served in the dining-room before the ladies retire. The prolonged wine-drinking now so generally condemned is thus discouraged. When the ladies retire, the gentlemen rise, and the gentleman nearest the door holds it open while the ladies pass out. For gentlemen to remain long after the ladies have gone is in bad taste and a poor compliment to the hostess and her fair guests. It is in still worse taste to rejoin them with flushed faces and uncertain speech. A refined gentleman is always temperate.

LENGTH OF A DINNER.

Speaking of the length of a good dinner, a recent writer quotes Napoleon the Third as insisting on being served in three-quarters of an hour. "As usual," says the writer in question, "here we run from one extreme to another. One of our most fashionable women boasted to me that she had dined out the day before, and the time consumed from the hour she left her house, until her return home, was but one hour and forty minutes. This is absurd. A lover of the flesh-pots of Egypt grumbled to me that his plate was snatched away from him by the servant before he could half get through the appetizing morsel on it. This state of things has been brought about by stately, handsome dinners, spun out to too great length. One hour and a half at the table is long enough.'

THE EYE SHOULD HAVE A FEAST.

In an interesting chapter on "Dinners," a popular authority says that "It is now the fashion to have the most superb embroidered table-cloths from Paris, in themselves costing nearly a year's income. But it is to be remembered that thirty years ago we imported from England the fashion of placing in the center of the table a handsome piece of square scarlet satin, on which to place the silver. At the dinner the eye should have a feast as well as the palate. A beautifully laid table is very effective. I have seen Her Majesty's table at Windsor all ready for her. I have heard her footmen, in green and gold, re-echo from hall to kitchen the note that 'dinner is served,' and then I was told to go; but I saw all I wanted to see. Her six footmen placed their hands on the little velvet Bishop's cap, which covered the lion and the unicorn in frosted gold on the cover of her six *entree* dishes; as dinner was announced, the velvet cap was removed."

A VEXED QUESTION.

An interesting point in dinner-party etiquette has been much discussed in high social circles. At a large dinner, where the only lady is the hostess, should she rise and receive each guest? This is still a vexed question. Again, at a large dinner of men, is it incumbent on every one present to rise on the entrance of each guest? "On one occasion," says the leader of the Four Hundred, "I failed myself to do this, not thinking it necessary. The distinguished man who entered said afterward that I had 'slighted him.' It was certainly unintentional. In a small room, if all get up, it must create confusion."

SOME GOLDEN RULES.

The literature of gastronomy is voluminous and interesting, and no one has written more entrancingly or with greater authority on the subject than Brillat Savarin, the great French epicure. His "Golden Rules of the Dinner Table" should be committed to memory. They are as follows:

"Let not the number of the guests exceed twelve, so that the conversation may be general. Let them be so selected that their occupation shall be varied, their tastes similar, their points of contact so numerous that to introduce them shall be scarcely necessary.

"Let the dining-room be superbly lighted, the cloth of exquisite fineness and gloss, the temperature of the room from 13 deg. to 16 deg. Reamur (60 deg. to 68 deg. Fahrenheit).

"Let the men be cultivated, without pretensions; and the ladies charming, without coquetry.

"Let the dishes be exceedingly choice, but not too numerous; and every wine first-rate of its kind.

"Let the order of the dishes be from the substantial to the light, and of wines from the simplest to those of richest bouquet.

"Let the business of eating be very slow, the dinner being the last act of the lady's drama; and let the guests and host consider themselves as so many travelers journeying leisurely toward the same destination.

"Let the coffee be hot and the liquors be chosen by the host.

"Let the drawing-room be large enough for a game of cards, if any of the guests cannot do without it, and yet have space enough remaining for after-dinner conversation.

"Let the guests be retained by the attractions of the party, and animated with the hope of some evening meeting again under the same pleasant auspices.

"Let not the tea be too strong; let the toast be buttered in the most scientific manner; let the punch be prepared to perfection.

"Let no one depart before 11 o'clock, and no one be in bed later than 12.

"If any one has been present at a party fulfilling these conditions, he may boast of having been present at his own apotheosis."

WHERE OLD RULES PREVAIL.

Where old customs are clung to and old fashions prevail in the service of dinner, the gentleman who supports the lady of the house should offer to relieve her of the duties devolving upon her. Many hostesses are well pleased thus to delegate the difficulties of carving, and all gentlemen who accept invitations to dinner should be prepared to render such assistance and do it gracefully. To offer to carve a dish and then perform the office unskillfully is an unpardonable *gaucherie.* Every gentleman should be able to carve and to carve well.

DUTIES OF HOSTESS.

The duties of hostess at a dinner party are not burdensome, but they demand tact and good breeding, grace of bearing and self-possession in no ordinary degree. She does not often carve, she has no active duties to discharge, but she must neglect nothing, forget nothing, put all her guests at their ease, and pay every possible attention to the requirements of each and all around her. Her temper must be kept under even the most trying accidents. She must let no disappointment disturb or embarrass her. She must see her old china broken without a sigh, and her best glass shattered with a smile.

DUTIES OF HOST.

But the duties of the host are not so light. A modern writer thus discourses on the host and his difficult role: "To perform faultlessly the honors of the table is one of the most difficult things in society. It might, indeed, be asserted, without much fear of contradiction, that no man has yet reached exact propriety in his office of host, or has hit the mean between exerting himself too much and too little. His great business is to put every one entirely at his ease, to gratify all his desires, and make him, in a word, absolutely contented with men and things. To accomplish this, he must have the genius of tact to perceive, and the genius of finesse to execute; ease and frankness of manner; a knowledge of the world that nothing can surprise; a calmness of temper that nothing can disturb; and a kindness of disposition that can never be exhausted. When he receives others, he must be content to forget himself; he must relinquish all desire to shine, and even all attempts to please his guests by conversation, and rather do all in his power to let them please one another. He behaves to them without agitation, without affectation; he pays attention without an air of'protection; he encourages the timid, draws out the silent and directs conversation without sustaining it himself. He who does not do all this is wanting in his duty as host; *he who does is more than mortal.*

BALLS.

BALLS.

The invitations to a ball must be sent out two or three weeks in advance. The number of guests depends somewhat on the size of your house and the length of your visiting list. Ordinarily the number invited is about twice what your rooms will hold, since some will not be able to accept, and others will fail at the last moment. During the height of the season this precaution is especially necessary, since many of the guests will be going to other balls and receptions, and you will naturally desire to insure the presence of a sufficiently large company throughout the evening. A hundred guests constitute a "ball;" over that, a "large ball;" under that, a "dance."

WALL-FLOWERS.

Only those who dance should accept invitations to a ball.

The presence of "wall-flowers" is not an honorable distinction which a hostess will crave.

ASSEMBLE AT 10 O'CLOCK.

Guests usually begin to assemble at a ball at 10 o'clock, but arrivals may continue till break of day, where attendance at other affairs has made an early appearance impossible.

RECEIVING GUESTS.

The lady of the house receives her guests at the door, supported by her husband. The sons assist in introducing the guests as they arrive, and the young ladies of the family busy themselves with keeping up the dances, but they must not dance until all their friends have been provided with partners.

GENTLEMAN ESCORTING LADY.

If a gentleman engages to escort a lady to a ball, he must call for her in a carriage at the hour appointed, and he is expected to send a bouquet in the course of the afternoon. Arrived at the house of the hostess, he escorts his fair charge immediately to the dressing-room, where he leaves her, going thence to the gentlemen's dressing-room, where he will make his own toilet as speedily as possible. He will then return to the ladies' dressing-room, waiting at the door till the lady appears, when he will escort her to the ball-room and immediately to the hostess.

GENTLEMAN UNACCOMPANIED BY. LADY.

Where a gentleman is unaccompanied by a lady, he must ask one of the young ladies of the house for the first dance. If she declines on the plea of want of room, or that some of her guests are without partners, he must gracefully yield, and lead out any lady the hostess may designate. Every gentleman must make a point of asking the ladies of the house to dance, and he must not selfishly slight those unfortunates who may have outlived their youth and beauty.

ETIQUETTE OF THE BALL-ROOM.

The lady, by the rules of etiquette, is obliged to dance the first dance with her escort, but after that she is at liberty to accept other partners. The gentleman, however, must be alert throughout the evening in her behalf, taking especial care that she is not neglected. He will escort her to supper, and hold himself in readiness to take her home at any moment she may elect.

SECURING PARTNERS.

A gentleman must select his partner before the music commences, and in leading her to and from the floor he must offer his arm, and not his hand.

When a lady has declined to dance on the score of fatigue, she must not be seen upon the floor again unless she has expressly stated that she wished to rest for that dance alone.

It is an unpardonable rudeness for a gentleman to turn directly from a lady who has declined to dance with him, to ask another, who has overheard the refusal. If the first lady has a prior engagement, it is the gentleman's duty to seek a partner in another part of the room, but where she pleads fatigue, or a disinclination to dance that set, he should pay her the compliment of remaining by her side till it is time to seek a partner for the next number.

No lady will dance with one gentleman after she has refused another. In declining to dance she must never do so point blank, but she may plead fatigue or some other reasonable excuse.

When a lady desires to sit down before the close of a dance her partner must not insist on her remaining on the floor. He must at once escort her to a seat, expressing his regret at the interrupted pleasure. But if she release him then he pays her a poor compliment if he go to seek another partner.

Ladies are expected to receive all introductions which may be proposed at a private ball, but at a public ball they may use their own judgment in the matter with perfect propriety.

A young lady should not dance with the same partner more than twice unless she desires to be noticed.

It is a rigorous rule that ladies must not enter or cross a ball-room without an escort.

Walking about the room after a dance is not permitted. The young lady is instantly returned to her seat when the music stops.

It is not in good form to make arrangements for another dance while one is in progress. Partners should be secured between the dances, and a lady should be extremely careful not to engage herself to two gentlemen for the same number. To forget an engagement is a shocking breach of good manners.

A gentleman in asking a lady to dance may do so in any polite form, but ordinarily he will say, " Will you honor me with your hand for a quadrille?" or "Shall I have the honor of dancing the next set with you ?"

Ladies who have danced every set should not boast of the fact in the presence of other ladies who may not have been so fortunate.

The Masquerade.

Ladies must not leave a ball-room alone.

Gentlemen may not ask a lady to dance unless a formal introduction has taken place.

SUPPER AT MIDNIGHT.

Supper is announced at midnight and the supper-room is kept open from that time till the ball closes. The gloves are removed at supper

ESCORTING LADY HOME.

When ready to withdraw, do so quietly, reserving your compliments and thanks to the hostess for a future occasion, when you should make a call for the express purpose of acknowledging your debt of gratitude for the pleasure you have enjoyed.

After a gentleman has escorted a lady home, he must on no account enter the house, even if invited to do so, but he should call on her the following afternoon or evening to pay his respects and inquire after her health.

ADDITIONAL HINTS.

It is not considered well-bred to stay too late at a ball. A gentleman must not take the vacant seat next to a lady unless he is acquainted with her, and not then without her express permission.

It rests entirely with the lady whether she recognize a ball-room acquaintance at a future meeting. If she doesn't care to do so she need not, and no gentleman will presume upon such an acquaintance.

Married people are not expected to dance with each othei at either a public or private ball.

Gloves of white kid must be worn throughout the evening.

At the beginning and end of a quadrille the gentleman bows to his partner, and again when he hands her to a seat

PRIVATE ENTERTAINMENTS.

PRIVATE ENTERTAINMENTS

Distinct from dinner-parties and balls are a number of morning and evening affairs which are known as conversaziones, private concerts, private theatricals, soirees, dramatic readings, tea-parties and matinees. These are usually somewhat less formal than either the dinner and the ball, but the same general rules of etiquette apply, modified to conform with the circumstances.

Under the head of conversaziones are included "Receptions" and "At Homes" and for these invitations should be issued a week or so in advance. At a conversazione, as the name implies, the chief feature is conversation, and, when literary or scientific people are thus drawn together, is the sole one, if we except the refreshments that the hostess is expected to serve. For ordinary occasions, however, especially where the guests are principally young people, the conversazione may be diversified by music, games and even impromptu dances.

RECEIVING THE GUESTS.

For small evening parties, the host and hostess, during the early part of the evening, remain near the door to receive the guests; but late-comers must not expect to find them in this position, for it becomes their duty, when the company, or the major portion of it, is assembled, to mix among the guests and provide for their entertainment. However, the host and hostess should be quick to note a late arrival and to make him welcome. As the guests enter the room, the hostess should advance a step or two to meet them, uttering a few words of greeting, first addressing the elder ladies, then the younger ones, and lastly the gentlemen. If the new-comers are strangers, the hostess must introduce them immediately to those present, but otherwise they must pass on, after a moment, leaving the hostess to look after later arrivals.

AVOID FUSSINESS.

A well-bred hostess will avoid fussiness. She will remain constantly with her guests and not fidget in and out as if she were busy with the supper or doubtful of her servants. She will have seen to all the details of supper and service before the company have come, and she will thus be able to appear in their eyes as one who has no thought beyond the reception-rooms and those who throng them.

ENTERTAINING.

At a formal conversazione it is desirable to have some person distinguished in art, literature, science, travel, war or politics; and he of course is the central figure about which all others revolve, but it will be well to invite some other notables who will in some degree divide attention with the star attraction.

HOSTESS SEES THAT CONVERSATION DOES NOT DRAG.

A hostess must not interrupt a *tete-a-tete* which is obviously interesting to the participants, but if she perceive that conversation languishes between a couple thrown together, she should skillfully bring a third into it, or adroitly draw one of the party away while substituting another.

MUSIC AND DANCING.

When dancing is introduced, the etiquette of the ball-room is the etiquette of the evening party. If the hostess cannot herself preside at the instrument, she should provide a pianist to furnish the music, rather than devolve upon any of her guests that duty. She certainly has no right to victimize a willing soul who may not like to refuse to play if asked. However, a gentleman who is a good pianist may, with entire propriety, offer his services to the hostess to play for an impromptu dance, or he may offer to relieve any lady so engaged, to give her an opportunity to join with those on the floor. If the ladies outnumber the gentlemen, however, and he is required to fill a set, he must not insist on playing, but rather remain where he is most needed.

ICES.

Ices alone are handed around once or twice during the evening at a dancing party, the supper being served later, if at all. As a rule, however, ices, lemonade, cake, confectionery and fruit are considered sufficient for a small evening party which breaks up early.

INVITING GUESTS TO SING OR PLAY.

When the party is mixed—that is, when it includes conversation, music and dancing—the hostess may invite her guests to sing or play, but if a guest declines, it is bad taste to insist on a compliance with the request. If the hostess herself sings or plays, she may favor the guests with a single selection after the others have been heard. A guest should not be asked to sing or play a second time, unless the company generally manifest a desire to that effect. Amateurs should make themselves the masters of at least a few pieces which they can render without the notes. To carry your music with you is to suggest that you expect to be asked to play or sing, and to go without them, unless you have learned something by heart, is to be forced to decline if called upon, the one case being as embarrassing as the other.

PRESERVING ORDER.

When one is playing or singing it is not polite to continue talking, at least in ordinary tones. If a companion insists on conversation, the voice should be subdued and you should withdraw from the immediate vicinity. But a singer or player will not wait for a lull in the room, or manifest annoyance, however galling the buzz of conversation, spoiling the finest effects, may be. Considerate people will never forget the feelings of others, however, and only those lacking in civility will disturb one who is making an effort to please.

GENTLEMAN ESCORTS LADY TO PIANO.

When a lady is invited by the hostess to sing or play, the gentleman nearest to her should offer his arm to escort her to the instrument, remaining near her during the performance and turning the music for her if he be competent.

He will also take charge of her fan, bouquet and gloves, and
when she is ready to return to her seat he must again offer
his arm, at the same time thanking her for the pleasure she
has afforded himself and others.

PLAYING AN ACCOMPANIMENT.

When one is asked to play an accompaniment, he should·
play, not to display his own talent, but so as to afford the
best possible support for the singer. This applies as well to
a second in an instrumental duet. It is well to remember
that a second is not the first.

PRIVATE THEATRICALS.

In giving private theatricals and concerts success can bₑ
secured only by making the performances very good. Indif·
ferent players or singers can produce only indifferent results,
and a hostess who attempts to entertain her friends by the
presentation of cheap talent must not be surprised if her
guests yawn instead of applaud. Wherever it is possible professional talent should be secured for private concerts, and
amateurs who consent to appear on the programme ought to
feel very confident of their abilities, even though none but
personal friends will be their auditors and critics.

CONVERSATION.

Between the parts conversation may be indulged in, but
during the performance guests must be seated and decorous
silence must prevail, broken only by the applause called for by
the merits of the numbers; but to hiss or otherwise manifest
disapproval of any private performance is utterly unheard of.

MAKING COMMENTS ON INSTRUMENTS.

A lady or gentleman who is asked to play will not make unfavorable comments on the instrument.   To do so is exceedingly rude.

TURNING THE MUSIC.

Persons who do not read music at sight should not offer to turn the leaves for a player, lest they cause confusion by turning too soon or too late.

HOSTESS MAKES THE PROGRAMME.

Unless she deputes the business to a stage manager, it is the duty of the hostess, in arranging for a private concert or theatricals—which latter includes charades, tableaux, proverbs and dramatic reading—to make up the programme and cast the parts.   Those selected by her to assist in the performance should show their appreciation of the honor by a cheerful acceptance of the parts assigned, even though such parts may be obscure or not just what they themselves would have chosen.   The arrangements of the hostess must be gracefully acquiesced in and the performer is in duty bound to acquit himself to the very best of his ability no matter how uncongenial his role may be.   But the hostess should consult each one before assigning the parts and try to suit all. Neither the host nor the hostess must take conspicuous parts in a performance unless urged to do so by the rest of those who are to participate in it.   When one has undertaken a part, only the gravest reasons will be accepted for its relinquishment.   No ordinary excuse will suffice and any failure to fulfill such an obligation is not only an insult to the hostess but an affront to the rest of the performers.

THE HOURS FOR PRIVATE THEATRICALS.

The hours usually selected for such entertainments are from 2 to 6 in the afternoon or from 8 to 11 in the evening. Ordinarily the programme is divided into two parts, and between these it is admissible for the spectators to promenade and otherwise to promote the social amenities of the occasion.

Full morning dress is most appropriate for matinees, which are usually held in the open air, and it is desirable to have a good brass band or an orchestra to furnish the music. No introductions are given, the guests pursuing their own devices and amusing themselves as best they may.

REFRESHMENTS.

If tents are not erected in the grounds selected, luncheon may be spread on tables under the trees, or even indoors. Cold meats, salads, fruits, ices and confections, with tea and coffee, should be served. Private fetes in the country correspond to matinees in the city, and the same general rules are applicable. Ceremony is laid aside on these occasions and people act with much greater freedom than at more formal gatherings.

GREAT TACT REQUIRED.

·In the management of a party, whether in the country or city, whether great or small, morning or evening, no little tact is required. The hostess must consult the tastes and wishes of her guests and let the knowledge thus gained be her guide. To compel a large party to listen to indifferent music or to watch the bungling performance of charades by two or three ambitious amateurs anxious to exhibit their talents is in bad taste, to say the least, and to suffer the younger members of a mixed assembly to dominate the entertainment is disrespectful to the older people and shows a want of consideration. As far as possible a company should be congenial in its elements, but this is often out of the question and it therefore becomes the duty of the hostess to arrange the programme so as best to suit the majority of her guests.

MUCH OF YOUR PLEASURE DEPENDS UPON YOURSELF.

"Your pleasure at any party," says a distinguished social authority, "will depend far more upon what you take with you into the room than upon what you find there. Ambition, vanity, pride, will all go with anxiety, and you will probably carry them all home again, with the additional burden of disappointment. Even if they are all gratified, you will know that others are disliking you, even if envious of you. To go with a sincere desire to please others by amiability, good-nature and sympathy will probably result in your own popularity and if you entirely forget yourself, you will be astonished to find how much others insist upon remembering you."

FUNERALS

Leaves have their time to fall
    And flowers to wither at the North Wind's breath,
And stars to set; but all,
    Thou hast all seasons for thine own,. O Death.
                        —*Felicia Hemans.*

There is no flock, however watched and tended.
    But one dead lamb is there.
There is no fireside, howsoe'er defended,
    But has one vacant chair.
                        —*Henry W. Longfellow.*

FUNERALS.

In the midst of life we are in death. Bishop Hall has said that "death borders upon our birth, and our cradle stands in the grave." And Shakespeare says that "nothing can we call our own but death, and that small model of the barren earth which serves as paste and cover to our bones." Dr. Young in his "Night Thoughts" declares that "death is the crown of life."

> "Were death denied, poor men would live in vain;
> Were death denied, to live would not be life;
> Were death denied, ev'n fools would wish to die."

Bryant calls death the Deliverer and says "God hath anointed it to free the oppressed and crush the oppressor." To Wordsworth death was "the quiet heaven of us all."

"O eloquent, just and mighty death!" exclaims Sir Walter Raleigh; "whom none could advise, thou hast persuaded; what none hath dared, thou hast done; and whom all the world have flattered, thou only has cast out of the world and despised: thou hast drawn together all the far stretched greatness, all the pride, cruelty and ambition of men, and covered it all over with these two narrow words, *Hic jacet?*" Byron was terrorized in the contemplation of death. He cries:

> "Oh, God! it is a fearful thing
> To see the human soul take wing
> In any shape, in any mood."

But to Longfellow

> "There is no death! What seems so is transition;
>   This life of mortal breath
> Is but a suburb of the life elysian,
>   Whose portal we call death."

Yet this transition is a solemn and fearful event and the boldest shrink in the presence of the Pale Horseman. But "men must endure their going hence, even as their coming hither." There is no escape. Some day the finger of God will touch us all and we shall sleep. "The shadow cloaked from head to foot, who keeps the keys of all the creeds," will fall upon us, and earth and its beauties, its joys and its sorrows, its interests and affections, will fade away into the impenetrable mysteries of eternity.

"Take a serious look at the world," exclaims an eloquent writer, "and what a piteous spectacle it presents! Imagine that you are standing outside, where you can look in at the world and upon the generations of men. You can see its joys and its sorrows, its triumphs and its defects; and being removed from the strifes and impulses of men you can judge impartially. To your view, the world would be one great funeral procession. Some are laughing, some crying, but all are moving toward the grave. Some are walking with slow steps, some bounding with light and joyous tread, some moving with stately bearing; but all carrying their burdens to the same place—the tomb. Funeral bells are tolling constantly. In one place a peasant is being borne to his humble resting-place. In another place, a steady procession, in all the pomp and splendor of earth, is bearing a king to the tomb. He, too, lays all his wealth and power and robes and even his crown at the open door of the grave. The pale boatman receives them both alike, and bears them to their home. One is not more distinguished than the other. Alike they cross the river, and alike they are received on the other shore so far as their earthly power and possessions are concerned. They take nothing with them except their wealth of soul and power of true manhood. And so do pauper and millionaire move steadily toward the same resting-place, each leaving his earthly possessions—the one his rags, the other his robes and palaces, at the door of the grave."

AN OCCASION OF SORROW.

In all ages death has been the occasion of sorrow and lamentation. Rachel wept for her children and when Job heard of the tragic death of his sons and daughters he "arose, and rent his mantle, and shaved his head, and fell down upon the ground; and his three friends made an appointment together to come to mourn with him and to comfort him. And when they lifted up their eyes afar off, and knew him not, they lifted up their voices and wept; and they rent every one his mantle and sprinkled dust upon their heads toward heaven. So they sat down with him upon the ground seven days and seven nights, and none spake a word unto him, for they saw that his grief was very great."

Here we have a striking picture of the ceremonial of mourning in the far East three thousand years ago. We

might add to this, pictures from more recent times illustrat-
ing the funeral customs and observances of people more
nearly akin to us in race and modes of thought. We might
refer to the ceremonials of the Greeks and the Romans.
reveal glimpses of the mystic Druid in his practice of strange
rites to the dead, and interest would not be waiting in a
sketch of the peculiar modes of mourning which travelers
have observed among the rude inhabitants of barbarous lands.
But space forbids and we must confine ourselves to some
brief hints on the etiquette of the funeral as custom has de-
termined it in our own country and in our own time.

AVOID TOO GREAT DISPLAY.

In England the hired mutes and the heavy trappings of
woe are still in vogue, but here, happily, these have been entirely discarded, the tendency being toward a simplicity that
better accords with the sentiments of real grief than all the
pomp and ostentation that circumstance ever convinced. To
surround the funeral ceremonies with great parade is usually
much more a vain display than an act of respect to the dead;
but if ostentation is to be avoided, so are meanness and parsi-
mony.

It is as deep an offense against the proprieties of life to
slight the dead as to slight the living; and while good taste
revolts against undue display, it demands that nothing shall
be done meanly or grudgingly.

The Grave.

FUNERAL DIRECTOR.

As death is the saddest of all events in each family, its occurrence calls for the sympathy of relatives and friends; and these owe duties which must be performed with delicacy and tact. The observance of forms which long usage has approved will lessen their own difficulties and in some measure relieve the natural grief of the bereaved, who must in all cases intrust, as far as possible, the details of the funeral to others, usually to a relative or near friend, who will proceed to make all required arrangements, thus sparing the family from many necessarily painful discussions and interviews. Where there is no relative or friend to undertake these duties, the whole matter of arrangements should be left in the hands of the funeral director, with such instructions as may be deemed proper, including the limit of expense, regulated by the wealth and position of the family.

ANNOUNCEMENT.

Announcement of the death may be made in the newspapers, with notice of the funeral arrangements. Funeral notices may also be printed and and sent around to the relatives and friends. The mails must not be used, except in reaching distant friends, the notices or invitations being delivered by special messenger.

ORDER OF CARRIAGES.

Should no invitations be issued the notice in the newspaper should read "without further invitation." In this case no especial order is required for the placing of guests, who

16

simply follow in the carriages after the members of the family. But where invitations have been formally issued, the funeral director should be supplied with a list of the invited guests in the order in which they are to be placed in the carriages.

ORDER AT FUNERALS.

It should be observed in the house of mourning that loud talking is an intolerable rudeness. Gentlemen upon entering must remove their hats and not replace them until in the open air again In the presence of death all enmities must be forgotten. Enemies who meet at a funeral are bound by etiquette to salute each other with quiet gravity.

While the dead remains in the house, the members of the bereaved family may deny themselves even to their nearest friends without offense and no casual visitor or friend must intrude upon their grief. It is proper that some relative not immediately connected with the family of the deceased should receive all callers and do the melancholy honors of the occasion.

DO NOT ARRIVE TOO EARLY.

Guests should not present themselves at a funeral before the hour appointed, the family paying their last sad visit to the coffin previous to that hour, when all intrusion upon them is a breach of propriety. The remains are ordinarily exposed in the parlor, the family congregating in another room.

VIEWING THE REMAINS.

When the period approaches for the final view, the funeral director will notify the family, who, after paying their last respects to the beloved dead, will immediately return to the apartment from which they issued and there remain until the ceremony has been concluded.

Where the services are held in a church, the remains are placed in front of the chancel. After the religious exercises the lid of the coffin is removed and the friends then pass slowly and reverently by, *from the feet to the head*, up one aisle and down another.

ORDER OF DEPARTURE.

After the services the clergyman leaves the house first, entering the carriage which precedes the hearse. Then follow the remains, after which comes the family, preceded by the funeral director. As they pass to their carriage, which immediately follows the hearse, guests and spectators must uncover. The funeral director assists the mourners into their carriage and then motions for the driver to move up, while the next carriage advances to receive its complement of guests, and so on till all who intend to follow the remains to the tomb have been seated. The cortege then moves, slowly in the country and in small towns, rapidly in large cities.

AT THE GRAVE.

When arrived at the place of sepulture the clergyman walks in advance of the coffin, while the guests assemble around the grave, those most nearly related to the deceased occupying the first places.

UNCOVERING THE HEAD.

In proceeding to the cemetery, if the friends go on foot, the gentleman may wear their hats, if the weather be cold or inclement; if the day be mild, it is customary to walk uncovered, with the hat held in the right hand. If the hat be worn, it must be removed as the coffin passes from the hearse to the church, or from the hearse to the grave, the guests forming a double line down which the pall-bearers pass with their burden.

THE USE OF FLOWERS.

The use of flowers at funerals is sometimes carried to an extravagant extent. Families now often, in giving notice of a funeral, add the significant phrase, "No flowers." But where ostentation is not the intent, nothing can be more beautiful or appropriate than a display of flowers, a variety of bloom, ranging from roses to pansies and from ivy to immortelles, being in favor. A wreath of pure white flowers is usually placed on the coffin of an infant or young person. Upon the coffin of one who has been married a cross of white flowers is appropriate. Around the coffin of a naval or army officer it is the custom to drape the national flag and upon it the hat, epaulets, sword and sash of the deceased are generally placed.

PALL-BEARERS.

In selecting pall-bearers the nearest friends of the deceased are usually designated. It is a foreign custom of much beauty and significance to select young children for pall-bearers for infants and children, attiring them in white and draping the coffin in white, trimmed with silver fringe and cords. When a young person dies the most intimate associates of the deceased are usually invited to act in the capacity of pall-bearers.

GLOVES AND CRAPE.

When gloves and crape bands are distributed to the gentlemen guests, they must be handed them as they enter the house; and it is considered a gross violation of etiquette to make any selection in such cases. The gloves given must be worn whether they fit the hands or not. But it is far better to provide yourself in advance with black kid gloves, permitting the funeral director to supply you with the crape only. Ladies in attending funerals must wear only the soberest garments.

VISITS OF CONDOLENCE.

It is not expected of friends in deep mourning that they will pay visits of condolence, and they are excused from accepting funeral invitations. But all others are expected to respond in such cases. It were a poor compliment to your friends whose dinners you have eaten, whose parties and balls you have attended and whose gayeties you have shared, to refuse to be present when they are in affliction, or to pay the last act of respect to the memory of one they love.

DEATH OF MEMBERS OF A SOCIETY.

When a member of any society dies, it is proper to notify the president thereof at once, who will then arrange with the master of ceremonies for any special marks of honor or observance which may be desired, always with the consent of the family.   In giving notice of the death of a member of any secret organization or fraternal order through the newspapers, care should be taken to specify the name of the society and the number of the lodge to which he belonged.   The regalia of the deceased is usually displayed on the coffin-lid, but it is removed before the remains are borne from the house.

ADDITIONAL NOTES.

When one has died of a contagious disease, invitations are not sent out and friends are not expected to attend the funeral.

Guests should not return to the house of mourning after the burial. A recent writer says that "in some sections it is customary to conclude the ceremonies of the day with a dinner or banquet, but this is grossly out of place and not to be tolerated by any one of common sense and refinement.   If friends have come from a distance, it may sometimes be a matter of necessity to extend a brief hospitality to them; but if the guests can avoid this necessity they should do so.   This hospitality should be of the quietest sort, and in no manner become an entertainment.   It is the cruelest blow which can be given bereaved friends to fill the house with strangers or indifferent acquaintances and the sound of feasting at a time when they desire of all things to be left alone with their sorrow.

MOURNING.

MOURNING.

On the subject of mourning observances a modern writer may be quoted: "Those who wish to show themselves strict observers of etiquette," he says, "keep their houses in twilight seclusion and sombre with mourning for a year or more, allowing the piano to remain closed for the same time. But in this close observance of the letter of the law its spirit is lost entirely.

"It is not desirable to enshroud ourselves in gloom after a bereavement, no matter how great it has been. It is our duty to ourselves and to the world to regain our cheerfulness as soon as we may, and all that conduces to this we are religiously bound to accept, whether it be music, the bright light of heaven, cheerful clothing, or the society of friends.

"At all events, the moment we begin to chafe against the requirements of etiquette, grow wearied of the darkened room, long for the open piano and look forward impatiently to the time when we may lay aside our mourning, from that moment we are slaves to a law which was originally made to serve us in allowing us to do unquestioned what was supposed to be in true harmony with our gloomy feelings.

"The woman who wears the badge of widowhood for exactly two years to a day, and then puts it off suddenly for ordinary colors, and who possibly has already contracted an engagement for a second marriage during these two years of supposed mourning, confesses to a slavish hypocrisy in making an ostentatious show of a grief which has long since died a natural (and shall we say a desirable?) death.

"In these respects let us be natural, and let us, moreover, remember that, though the death of friends brings us real sorrow, yet it is still a time of rejoicing for their sakes."

PERIOD OF MOURNING.

A French widow wears mourning during a period of fifty-eight weeks. For six months she wears deep mourning, the succeeding six months she wears ordinary mourning, During the remaining six weeks half-mourning is the rule; then she emerges in the usual colors prescribed by fashion.

For a father, mother or wife the French go into mourning for half a year—three of deep and three of half-mourning. For a sister or brother the period is two months, half of which is marked by deep mourning. A grandparent's death is marked by two and half months of slight mourning. Ordinary mourning is worn for three weeks in memory of an uncle or aunt, while for a cousin it is worn but for a fortnight.

In this country the rules are not so well-defined; but usually widows wear mourning for two years. In rare cases they retain their weeds during life. For parents the period of mourning is also two years, relieved somewhat during the latter half. For brothers and sisters deep mourning is worn for one year and lighter mourning for another year or less.

Uncles, aunts and grandparents are remembered by ordinary mourning during a period of three or six months. In many cases mourning is not worn at all except in memory of the nearest and dearest relatives. Parents sometimes wear mourning for a period of two years for grown-up sons and daughters, but it is not considered in the best taste to assume the trappings of woe for young children.

SECLUSION FROM SOCIETY.

One in deep mourning does not go into society, nor receive or pay visits. The utmost seclusion is demanded. Six months after the death of a near relative one may go to the theatre, but concerts may be attended at the expiration of three months.

GENTLEMEN IN MOURNING.

Gentlemen usually confine their signs of mourning to a band of crape on the hat. They do not exclude themselves from society for any long period, yet it is considered indecent for them to show haste in returning to the gay world after a serious bereavement. In rare cases the man who has lost his wife wears mourning for two years, but usually a much shorter period is deemed sufficient.

CHILDREN IN MOURNING.

It is neither good taste nor good sense to trick children out in the habiliments of grief. It is an injustice to them and it savors more of ostentation than of actual sorrow. And it is in equally bad taste to put servants into mourning. The custom might once have been honored, but it is no longer more than an empty form.

ADDITIONAL NOTES.

A superstition may be mentioned in this connection. It is, that it portends ill-luck when any guest appears at a wedding in a black dress. Hence, even those in deep mourning on the occasion of a marriage lay it aside for the moment and wear white, gray, purple or something else that is brighter than the somber insignia of grief.

Oculists are beginning to forbid the black veil as an injury to the eye. It also injures the skin, and by rubbing against the forehead and nose it often produces abrasions that develop troublesome sores. It is, therefore, falling gradually into disuse, except for brief periods of mourning.

Mourning should be discarded, not by a sudden change, but gradually.

CALLS AND VISITS.

CALLS AND VISITS.

Visiting occupies a very conspicuous place among the duties which social intercourse involves, and the etiquette of visiting is not to be slighted. In the cities visits of ceremony are a much more prominent social feature than in the country towns, but even in the latter there are formal morning calls, visits of condolence and congratulation, "party calls" and the like, that society more or less rigidly requires of its votaries.

MORNING CALLS.

The morning call is not a morning call at all, because it is paid in the afternoon, between the hours of 3 and 5—late enough to clear the luncheon hour and too early to interfere with the dinner. A visit before noon is not tolerated by the *haut ton,* and it is considered a very awkward thing to time a call so that the family will be disturbed in either their luncheon or dinner arrangements.

RETURNING VISITS.

It is a social rule that first visits shall be returned, if not the next day, at least within three days ; and these visits must always be brief, in no case running over half an hour, no matter how delightful the conversation may be.

VISITS OF CEREMONY.

A visit of ceremony may be returned simply by leaving your card at the door, without entering. It is proper, however, to inquire after the health of the family. Where the lady upon whom you call has daughters or sisters in the house, it is expected that a card will be left for each; and if there be visitors there, it is better to distinguish the cards intended for them by writing their names above your own. A married lady who calls upon a married lady leaves her husband's card for the husband of her friend. It is not allowable to send cards around by a servant except in returning thanks for "kind inquiries" and in announcing your departure from or your arrival in town.

Within a week after the event a call should invariably be made at a house where you have dined, or have been invited to dine. Visits of congratulation are to be made in person and it is not only required that you shall go in, but that you shall be hearty in expressing your good-will and good wishes. Those who have received wedding cards are supposed to be those with whom the newly-married pair desire to maintain friendly relation, and these call first. Guests at a wedding feast must also call on the parents who gave it.

NEVER KEEP VISITOR WAITING.

A lady should never keep a visitor waiting. If a caller has been admitted, in the absence of any instruction to the servant that you are "not at home," you are obliged to receive the visitor at any sacrifice of personal convenience.

GENTLEMEN'S MORNING CALLS.

When gentlemen make morning calls, they carry their hats with them into the room and retain them in their hands or place them on the floor. Overcoats and umbrellas are always left in the hall. It is not in good taste to let your dog follow you into the drawing-room when you make a morning call. He may in obvious ways prove annoying. Nor should a mother take young children with her on such visits.

PAYING RESPECTS TO HOSTESS FIRST.

When one enters a crowded drawing-room, it is proper to go at once to the lady of the house, to whom the visitor must pay his respects, after which the guest is seated in the chair indicated by the hostess.

INTRODUCTIONS.

When introductions are given it is only necessary to bow, except in the case of near friends or relations of the hostess, when you may offer your hand. A gentleman has no right to take a lady's hand till it is offered. A lady gives her hand to a gentleman, but does not shake his hand in return. Young ladies only bow to unmarried men. On the entrance of ladies a gentleman is expected to rise, but ladies remain seated. A gentleman also rises when any lady takes her leave. If he is in his own house, he escorts her to her carriage.

DEPARTING.

If you are on the point of departure when other visitors are announced, wait till they are seated; then take leave of the hostess, bow politely to the new arrivals, and retire. It is not well to resume your seat after having once started to go. A visitor may consult his watch only after apologizing for the act on the ground of other engagements.

DUTIES OF HOSTESS.

A lady receiving morning visits is not required to lay aside the work on which she may be engaged, except it be of an absorbing character, like music or drawing. Light needle work may be continued without impropriety. The hostess need not advance to receive visitors, unless as a mark of special cousideration. It is deemed sufficient if she rise, take a step or two forward and shake hands with them, and remain standing till they have been seated. She will pay equal attention to her guests, keeping the conversation as general as possible. If one of the visitors is particularly famous it is allowable to give him extra consideration, but as a rule all must receive equal notice and equal courtesy. When the visitors rise to leave, the lady of the house rises also and remains standing until they have left the room. A servant is expected to be ready to show them out.

HINTS ON DRESS.

The subject of dress for making or receiving morning calls might be dilated upon, but it will be sufficient to suggest a lady should be well but not too richly attired on such occasions. If a lady is calling in a carriage it is of course permissible for her to array herself in a more elegant costume than she would wear were she on foot. Gentlemen must always dress well.

VISITS OF FRIENDSHIP.

But there are visits of a less formal character which deserve attention. These are visits of friendship, more or less prolonged, during which the guest becomes a member of tho family whose hospitality he enjoys.

IN ENGLAND.

In England this sort of visiting has probably reached the stage of poetical perfection and Trollope and other British novelists have made us familiar with all its amenities. Byron has also given us a picture of guest life in an English country house in the following stanzas:

> The gentlemen got up betimes to shoot,
>   Or hunt; the young, because they like the sport.
> The first thing boys like, after play and fruit;
>   The middle-aged to make the day more short;
> For *ennui* is a growth of English root,
>   Though nameless in our language—we retort
> The fact for words, and let the French translate
> That awful yawn which sleep cannot abate.
>
> The elderly walked through a library,
>   Or troubled books, or criticised the pictures,
> Or sauntered through the garden piteously,
>   And made upon the hot-house several strictures;
> Or rode a nag which trotted not too high,
>   Or in the morning papers read their lectures;
> Or on the watch their longing eyes would fix,
> Longing at sixty for the hour of six.
>
> But none were "gene;" the great hour of union
>   Was wrung by dinner's knell! till then all were
> Masters of their own time—or in communion,
>   Or solitary, as they chose to bear

The hours, which how to pass to few is known.
　Each rose up at his own, and had to spare
What time he chose for dress, and broke his fast
When, where, and how he chose for that repast.

HOSPITALITY.

Hospitality on the lavish scale of the English country house is rarely possible in the United States, but hospitality of the quieter sort is an American characteristic. Everybody has a visitor now and again, and every-body as far as his means will allow entertains with liberality and fine feel-, ing.

When a friend is invited to pay you a visit, you should name a season when you can devote at least a considerable portion of your time to his entertainment. When he arrives, he should be met at the station, if possible by the host himself. A special room should be reserved for the guest; and to this he should be shown as soon as the first greetings and civilities have been exchanged. No one should be allowed to enter this room uninvited; and every possible convenience and comfort should be provided, even to writing materials and stamps.

DUTIES OF GUEST.

But the guest should as far as may be adjust himself to the order of the household, giving the least possible trouble and entering with easy adaptability into the usual courses of the family, observing its religious practices, adopting its hours and in all ways avoiding friction or the suggestion of singularity. Punctuality at meal times is especially enjoined. To keep a whole family waiting for one at breakfast is a poor way to win their good-will. After breakfast the guest must expect to be left pretty much to his own devices until noon, when the hostess will be at liberty to give him some attention, but meanwhile she must have put him in the way of such self-amusement or employment as piano, billiard table or library may afford, and the guest must make the best of these resources.

When a lady is visiting she may very properly offer to assist her hostess about household duties; but it is not advisable to insist upon giving your help if the hostess seems disinclined to accept it.

A lady visitor may very properly employ herself in making some small ornament, such as a piece of embroidery, a sofa-cushion or piano-cover, to be presented to the hostess when finished as a memento of the visit. A gentleman visitor may gracefully compliment his hostess by occasional presents of fruit, flowers and confectionery. If there is a baby in the family some little gift to it will be mightily appreciated by the family.

A visitor must always be ready to ride, drive, walk, go to church, theatre or party, as his host and hostess may seem to desire; but they should be careful not to thrust upon a guest anything that may be distasteful. In fact, the guest's tastes should never be disregarded.

Letters should not be opened by a visitor in the presence of the family or other guests without begging their permission. The servants must not be needlessly troubled by a guest, but they may be asked to wait upon him as if they were his own. He should keep his room in an orderly condition and avoid leaving his things lying about to give trouble.

ENTERTAINING GUEST.

However, the host and hostess should give up as much of their time as they can to the amusement of a guest, yet over-attention is a danger to be studiously avoided. It is their duty to take the guest to any points of interest in the neighborhood and to invite any other friends he may have in the place to call on him and take tea or dine, the fact that such friends may be unknown to the host and hostess making no difference.

Outside engagements and visits must not be made without consulting the host and hostess, whose house you must not mistake for a hotel. Neither hostess nor guest may ac. cept invitations that do not include both, and if either is in mourning, all invitations must be declined by both during the visit.

ADDITIONAL HINTS.

The following additional hints and suggestions in relation to calls will be found useful.

If some good fortune has come to a friend, whether promotion in employment or a striking success in business, it is permissible to pay him a visit of congratulation, even though your last call has not been returned.

A visitor is not expected to draw near the fire unless invited to do so by the hostess. The caller must remain in the seat to which he has been assigned even at the price of phys-ical discomfort.

When visiting one who is sick you must not offer to go to the invalid's room until invited to do so. If you have received calls during an illness of your own, either in person or by card, you are required to return them as soon as you have sufficiently recovered to go abroad.

Staring about the room when calling is extremely rude, and one must not walk around looking at books or pictures or touch the piano while waiting for the hostess. Nor must a caller open nor shut a door, raise or lower a window, or in any way interfere with the arrangements of the room.

Visits made to friends in the country may be longer and less ceremonious than those in town.

Always avoid turning your back upon any member of a company.

The hostess must never leave the room while callers are in it.

The presence of a clock in a drawing-room is objected to as a too suggestive hint to callers to note the flight of time.

Visits of condolence should be made in sober attire and frivolous subjects as well as the discussion of the latest ball or opera should be avoided. Nor should the recent sorrow be discussed except on the mention of the mourner.

A call must never be prolonged until the next meal time. A visitor has no right to enforce an invitation to dinner or to tea.

A gentleman must never prolong a call when he finds

his host or hostess dressed to go out, even if urged to do so. He should remain only long enough to exchange the ordinary civilities of a brief visit and then retire with a promise to repeat the call in the near future.

It is an inflexible rule that a lady may not call upon a gentleman in a social way, except in the case of confined invalidism. She may go to see him on business or to get his professional advice, but not otherwise.

CONVERSATION.

The firste vertue, sone, if thou wilt lere,
Is to restreine, and keepen wel thy tonge.
                                        —*Chaucer.*

CONVERSATION.

"Syllables govern the world," said the great Selden, and the justice of the saying was nowhere made clearer than in the mighty career of Napoleon, who was not alone a man of action but one of speech. His tongue was scarcely less powerful than his sword, for while with the one he was invincible before his enemies, he was with the other the master of his friends. No one can read his impassioned speeches to his soldiers in Africa, in Italy, in Germany, in Russia, without catching something of the spirit with which they must have been inspired. Such prodigies of valor as Frenchmen displayed at Jena and Austerlitz were the fitting answer in action to the burning words of their beloved general. He won them first with his eloquence and then he won his battles. And so with Rienzi the Roman. His powers of speech were marvelous, and at the last his enemies refused to hear him because "his tongue would charm away their senses." They dared not listen to him, so irresistible was his eloquence. Syllables do indeed govern the world. Those of the old Greek orators still ring in the ears of mankind, still their charm controls the spirits and the acts of men; and still from Socrates and Plato we borrow the thoughts that undergird philosophers and creeds.

It has been said that the newspaper has destroyed the

orator, the letter-writer and the conversationalist at once; and there is too much truth in the statement, especially as it relates to the latter two. Oratory is still a powerful force, but it must be admitted that people will not always go to hear a speech which they can read the next morning at their breakfast-tables. Thus the practice of oratory is discouraged and the man with a gift of speech sits down to acquire the art of writing, so that he may command an audience. The letter-writer was once an important factor. Genius found vent through "Letters to Stella." Leigh Hunt cultivated letter-writing as a fine art, and soldiers, statemen, jurists and scholars alike courted fame through the medium of correspondence. But nobody writes letters to-day. If one has a thought in his head, he writes an article for the *North American* or the *Century* or his favorite paper. He does not develop it in a friendly epistle that the recipient is expected to pass around among a select coterie. Nor is the conversationalist what he once was when the *salon* was to France what the tribune was to Rome and what the Paris newspaper is to-day—the molder of public opinion. Yet in spite of the revolution which modern journalism has wrought, the art of conversation is by no means a lost one and he who can talk well is still an object of admiration and an influential factor of society. He shines where others only glimmer, and he gravitates to the center of every group as naturally as water runs down hill.

But no one can hope to succeed in conversing well without training. In the old days the wits went to the drawing-room or the *salon* with mature thought. Their sallies were planned out beforehand, as the orator plans his speech. They saturated themselves with some subject, or with several subjects which they expected to come up or meant to bring up on their own motion; and thus they were able to carry things off with great brilliancy and with an air of spontaneity that might very well deceive all but the initiated. Nowadays this sort of thing is not so prevalent, principally, it may be ventured, because there is not a very large leisure class. Most men are busy all day. They have precious little time for anything but their affairs, and when they go into society at the close of business they carry with them scarcely more than their general stock of information, and upon this they must draw at sight for every demand of conversation.

AN ENTERTAINING TALKER THE RESULT OF STUDY.

Hence the importance of a broad foundation of general culture for one who expects to build a reputation as a talker. An extensive reading, a close observation of men and manners, a varied experience, will give even a naturally dull man the power to entertain, so that the absence of wit and lively fancy will scarcely be noted. But pedantry is always to be avoided and modesty must ever be cultivated—where it is not an inherent quality—for, as Dr. Addison has said, "a just and reasonable modesty sets off every great talent a man may be possessed of. It brightens all the virtues which it accompanies; like the shades in paintings, it raises and rounds every figure and makes the colors more beautiful, though not so glaring as they would be without it." But in being modest you are not to be timid. Self-respect and confidence in one's own powers should give one boldness without egotism, assurance without impertinence, and vigor without rudeness. One's own discretion should be one's tutor.

> "But know that nothing can so foolish be
> As empty boldness; therefore first essay
> To stuff thy mind with solid bravery;
> Then march on gallant, yet substantial worth
> Boldness gilds finely, and will set it forth."

A forward man is usually one and he is always disagreeable. He thrusts himself in where wiser ones would hesitate to venture and thus excites the disfavor of those he aims to charm. "My son," said Parmenio the Grecian, "would you be great, you must be less; that is, you must be less in your own eyes if you would be great in the eyes of others." And a witty Frenchman observes that "the modest deportment of really wise men, when contrasted with the assuming air of the young and ignorant, may be compared to the different appearance of wheat, which while its ear is empty holds up its head proudly, but as soon as it is filled with grain, bends modestly down and withdraws from observation."

A FULL MIND AND CONFIDENCE.

Yet if forwardness is to be condemned and modesty studiously practiced, diffidence is to be overcome. The diffident man is often full of merit, but he obscures his own light by retiring it behind a bashful reserve. Such a man needs to arouse his own courage. He needs to face the difficulties in his way and to surmount them, acquiring strength and confidence as he presses forward. He may never be able to talk brilliantly, but if he accustoms himself to polite intercourse, keeping a full mind for the tongue to draw upon, he may at least become both interesting and agreeable in his conversation.

But Socrates himself could have talked but indifferently had he been surrounded by indifferent listeners.

> "A poet's prosperity lies in the ear
>   Of him that hears it, never in the tongue
>   Of him that makes it."

THE ART OF LISTENING.

A few conversationalists may have the power to compel attention, but the average talker cannot hope to do so. He must trust to the politeness of his audience, and therefore the art of listening well is not a misprized one. A good listener is sure to be agreeable to those who do the talking; and one who shows inattention is sure to offend. It is not enough merely to sit silent while another relates a story or expresses a conviction; there must be attention in the eye and in the face, emphasized by an occasional interjection of surprise, assent or encouragement. That one shall be able thus to win favor implies an actual following of the speaker's narrative or discourse, but it is a very hard thing for one to do. We are too prone to think only of what we mean to say ourselves when our time comes to give close heed to the arguments of another. Hence there arise confusion, misunderstanding, perhaps anger. The speaker who has stated his convictions clearly on a given point does not like the next man to proceed on the assumption that there has been evasion or that the other holds different convictions from those he expressed. Such an assumption would show either that the second speaker had not been listening or that he doubted the veracity of the first one, and the latter in either case would justly feel offended.

Hence, the wisdom of cultivating the habit of close attention to others in conversation. It is better, perhaps, that you should drop the thread of your own argument, or forget the point of your own story, while listening to another, than to wound him by inattention.

PROPER SUBJECTS FOR CONVERSATION.

But one must have something to talk about before undertaking to talk, so the question arises, What are proper subjects for polite conversation? Intimate friends may discourse as they please on any topic soever that may be agreeable or interesting, "from grave to gay, from lively to severe." They may talk of politics, religion, the weather, the last ball, the newest fashion, the play, the opera, even their own personal concerns. But in general company conversation is usually less latitudinal. Politics and religion are too liable to occasion heat to be safely introduced for discussion in a mixed company; the weather grows hackneyed, the last ball may not be a matter of interest to some, others may have their scruples about the stage; the fashions will scarcely enlist the

Earnest Conversation.

attention of the men, and personal affairs certainly cannot be brought on parade.

Where a conversational lion is present, he, of course, will set the paces. He will lead the conversation and give it the liveliest turns, drawing out the rest with skill, interspersing anecdote with story and sentiment, and diversifying the whole with wit and humor. Slander and gossip in any case will be avoided; each will add what he can to the feast of reason and flow of soul. And here is where one's reading, observation and experience will come to his aid One happy comment, a single apt illustration, will often grace a conversation more than a clever story, and an agreeable representation may thus be made. "Small talk," if not spiced with scandal, as small talk is too apt to be, is always to be preferred in a general company to heavy discourse, in which some may not be interested and others will not feel themselves able to join. Of course hard and fast rules cannot be laid down in a matter of this kind. Every gathering will suggest its own topics, each company will be governed by the tastes and the surrounding of its members, but no matter who the talkers may be or where they are met, they are bound to respect each other's feelings and preserve their own dignity.

AVOID TALKING SHOP.

Men will ordinarily avoid talking "shop." That is to say, the lawyer will not bring a brief, the clergyman will not fetch a sermon, or the doctor a lecture to inflict on the rest. Yet each may make his special knowledge useful without

13

bringing it on parade. It is a compliment to them to draw them out, but it is none to force them to deliver a lecture on law, theology and medicine, respectively. It would be quite proper to ask the physician what he thought of Dr. Koch's discovery, but he should not be expected to detail his views of bacteriology. The preacher might be asked his opinion of Andover Case, but to press him upon disputed doctrinal points might be embarrassing. And so the lawyer may be asked his view of a proposed piece of legislation, or of a pending suit of national or general interest, but to drag him into a discourse on constitutional law or civil practice would be unkind to him and inconsiderate, perhaps, of other members of the company—the banker, the merchant, the teacher, the architect and the writer, who may themselves want to be heard.

CAREFULLY AVOID YOUR "HOBBY."

The man with a hobby ought to look after himself very closely, else in conversation he will become a bore. So with those people—particularly ladies—who have "a mission.' Mrs. Jellaby had "a mission," but that did not prevent her from being disagreeable. It is a good thing for one to have a purpose in life, to believe in something, and to believe in it, too, with all one's might; but nevertheless one cannot expect one's friends or casual acquaintance to feel one's own enthusiasm and undivided interest in that thing, whatever it may be. Hence, it is wise to keep one's hobby in the background; and it is wholesome for one who is wedded to one idea to hear what those who entertain other ideas may have to say.

WIT THAT WOUNDS.

Ridicule is a powerful weapon in skillful hands; a dangerous one in those unskilled; but always a weapon that is out of place in a drawing-room or parlor, where it is not easy to guess who will be hurt if it is flourished. It were better to appear dull than to gain notice by the display of wit that wounds and leaves a scar. And it is always in bad taste to jest on sacred or solemn subjects; it is positively inexcusable to make a member of the company the victim of a joke, even if it be an innocent one. He will probably not enjoy being laughed at and jeered at better than you would yourself, and you know how well you like to be laughed at!

DO NOT INTERRUPT A SPEAKER.

Avoid any interruption of one who is speaking as you would have others avoid an interruption of yourself. In other words, apply the Golden Rule, which, if it have no place in politics, is not to be dispensed with in polite society, where the rights of others must be always your first and most important consideration.

MANNER OF SPEAKING.

The successful talker, like the successful orator, will speak neither too rapidly nor too slowly. A full, rich, musical tone should characterize the manner of speaking, avoiding all affectations, either of pronunciation or style. To clip your words of their due proportions or to mouth them like a third-rate actor is equally objectionable; and to "spout" is abominable.

THINKING TWICE.

Think twice before you speak. A careless word, an ill-considered statement, may react upon ycu like a boomerang, even if it do not injure the feelings or mis'ead the judgment of others. You cannot be too scrupulous in this respect; and the habit of a rapid survey and quick calculation of relations, effects and contingencies should be cultivated.

Dogmatism may be quite in place in the schools, but it is decidedly out of place in the drawing-room. Hence, even your convictions should be asserted with modesty and with a due regard for the opinions of others.

KEEP YOUR TEMPER.

An even temper is a powerful advantage in an argument; therefore, do not suffer yourself to become heated in discussion. If you lose your temper you will almost certainly lose your case; and besides that, you will lose the good opinion of the company while adding to the triumph of your opponent.

Do not too often "speak your mind," by which injunction we do not mean to discourage you in veracity, but merely to warn you against a not uncommon fault, that of detraction. When one "speaks his mind" about another he is too apt to vent his spleen; and that is something he should do in the privacy of his own chamber, if at all.

DO NOT COMMENT ON INFIRMITIES OF OTHERS.

The infirmities of others must be sacred from reflection or remark. To comment on the eccentricity or the peculiar weakness of any member of the company is not only an insult to him, but an outrage on good manners which every one will be justified in resenting. But if by inadvertence or carelessness you should inflict a wound, make instant apology, and show afterward that you sincerely regret the injury you have done.

THE ABJECT MAN.

The abject man is hardly less disagreeable than the over-bearing man, and he is certainly not so much entitled to re-spect, for the craven of all men is most despicable. Hence, to cringe before one who may be your superior in position, intel-lect or attainments is to invite contempt, as the display of arrogance to an inferior is to provoke resentment; and both are equally to be avoided.

MODERATION IN YOUR EXPRESSIONS.

Reserve your powers. To expend them to the utmost is to expose yourself to many unpleasant risks.

Self-praise, according to the old saw, is half scandal. Therefore leave your friends to praise you, while you praise them for any deserving. But let not praise degenerate into flattery, which is the food of fools. Defoe said that when flatterers meet the devil goes to dinner; and Shakespeare calls flattery the bellows that blows up sin. It is certainly an unpleasing vice and he who indulges in it is not worthy of honest men's regard.

Lord Bacon said that no pleasure is comparable to the standing upon the vantage ground of truth. But it is some-times wise to pause short of telling all the truth, though not one word you utter should be false. Yet if telling half the truth should convey the impression of a whole lie, either tell no part of it or else all of it.

When another is telling a story it is impertinent to correct him in details or to interrupt him in any way. Let him tell it in his own way even if that way is a very poor one in comparison with yours.

Do not seek differences in a company in which you happen to be. Rather look for points of agreement and avoid contention.

It sometimes happens that one is thrown into company which, socially, may be considered above him. He should in such case preserve a modest and dignified reserve. If drawn into the conversation on equal terms, he should not take it as an act of condescension. Should an individual slight him, let him quietly drop a conversation with the individual. If the company slight him, let him withdraw.

ADDITIONAL HINTS.

Don't indulge in unkindly witticisms. They leave bitterness behind.

Don't parade your learning, lest you be set down as a pedantic fool.

Don't undertake to reprove unless compelled to, and then do it with gentleness, avoiding needless offense.

Don't talk of things that the company do not incline to hear about. You may compel them to listen, but you can't keep them from thinking less of you.

Don't trumpet forth your own fame. Leave others to discover your merits and magnify your name.

Don't be tedious. Speak what you have to say tersely, with vivacity and directness. Sluggishness in conversation is intolerable.

Don't despise the man who knows less than yourself. His range of knowledge, humble as it may be and narrow, may possibly include a few things that you would do well to learn from him.

Don't offer gratuitous advice. You may be wise in your own conceit, but officiousness may meet with just resentment. If your advice be sought, give it with caution, after mature deliberation and under reservation. It is so easy for one to advise a false step where all the ground is not thoroughly known.

Don't assume the *role* of prophet, for it is the unexpected which happens. The ignorant foretell all events, but the wise are content to await in patience what the future may bring forth.

Don't talk too much; still waters deepest run. And on the other hand don't be a clam. The man who says nothing at all has only one-tenth as much to repent of, perhaps, as the man who says a great deal more than he should, yet he is not without reproach if he fail to add his quota to the sum of pleasant conversation.

Don't hold forth like an oracle. You may be one, it is true, but people nowadays have some difficulty in overcoming their skepticism on the subject of oracles. Always remember that wisdom will not die with you and cultivate a becoming sense of your own littleness as compared with this great populous world.

Don't assume the task of criticism. It is a thankless one, and if you unwisely undertake it you will find that the weak will fear and hate you, while the strong show resistance and contempt.

Don't accentuate your oddities, but seek to soften them down. Some men mistake eccentricity for individuality; but if they delude themselves they must not expect to delude others.

Don't hesitate to admit that you are in the wrong if you have found yourself so. Obstinacy in argument is not a merit nor is shiftiness a thing of which to be proud.

Don't enter an argument unless you mean to follow it out till you reach the truth. To dodge and equivocate and confuse the issue may be smart, but it is not manly or honorable.

Don't provoke any man if you can help it. Bear with the weaknesses and foibles of your neighbor, and if he seek to provoke you, don't suffer him to succeed. Keep calm and cool and know that thus you have an advantage.

Don't forget that the ladies are not over-fond of discussion. They usually prefer sentiment to logic and compliments to argumentation. So when they are present do not let the conversation take on a tone that will be unpleasant to their taste.

LETTERS.

LETTERS.

The "ready letter writer," with all its stilted forms and ceremonious absurdities, has happily gone out of whatever fashion it once enjoyed; and men and women now write as they talk—with naturalness, individuality and a sensible adaptation of style and form to the subject and the occasion. Certainly nothing could be more absurd than some of the high-flown epistles which have been handed down as models for young men and maidens since Lord Chesterfield's day, their fine words, rounded sentences and ponderous sentiment striking the modern ear with a delicious sense of the ridiculous and an equally delicious sense of the far-fetched and the archaic.

THE MODERN STYLE.

The modern style of letter-writing gains in force what it loses in circumlocution and ceremony. It is characterized by directness and brevity. Phrase is not piled on phrase. Words of learned length and thundering sound, so dear to the epistolary writer of the last century, are no longer in favor, plain, vigorous, Anglo-Saxon, free from affectation and absurdity, making a happy contrast between the new and the old. And thus has come an improvement in correspondence that accords with improvements in other directions. We write what we mean, using the simplest words and the fewest sentences for conveying the ideas we wish conveyed. Nor are we careless in our spelling, our punctuation or our grammar. In these particulars our ceremonious ancestors were by no means over-nice. They abbreviated shockingly; they spelled with the greatest freedom; their punctuation was indifferent; in grammar they were rather weak, to say the least, and some of them scrawled worse than a modern school-boy.

To-day we give attention as well to the mechanical as to the intellectual composition of our letters. We insist upon proper spelling, proper punctuation grammatical correctness and clear chirography. It is to lawyers only that an illegible hand-writing is allowed—and even to the victims of these has come relief through the type-writer, which is as merciless to the graphic faults of the author of a letter as it is merciful to one who is expected to read it. A bad penmanship often obscures other grievous faults; and it may sometimes be suspected that one who affects a wretched hand does so the better to conceal his ignorance of the Queen's English.

PENMANSHIP.

But be this as it may, the fact remains that one of the essentials of letter writing is a fair penmanship. The clerkly hand is not one to be cultivated for ordinary correspondence, since it is too suggestive of boxes and bales, or dry as dust parchments and papers. Nor is the stiff, formal hand, like that of a school master, one that you should suffer yourself to acquire. Rather let individuality in style and freedom in the movements of your pen characterize your chirography, yet always aiming at legibility and graceful form. Flourishes, heavy shadings, back slopings, and all that sort of thing, should be left to writing masters and to vain young men who choose to exhibit their talents in that peculiar way.

STATIONERY.

It has been elsewhere mentioned that ruled paper is allowable only in business correspondence. But perhaps for those whose lines have an up-hill or down-hill tendency, it were better to write even small notes on ruled sheets than to invite criticism by the other fault.

For notes, invitations and ordinary correspondence, plain paper is always preferable to the fancy styles that come and go in fashion. A good quality should always be chosen, either white or some delicate tint, say of cream, azure or pink. Odd shapes, colors and textures of course may be used when such becomes the rage; but while there is always some danger of offending against good taste by using fancy figure paper, there is never any risk in the employment of the plain white article, if thick and of choice quality. Envelopes should match the paper in all cases, in size, color and quality. Long letters of a friendly nature may properly be written on the French water lined papers; but these are too light for formal notes and the like. Monograms on paper and envelopes were once quite popular, but are no longer so, though still fancied by some. Ladies sometimes have facsimile copies of their initials placed diagonally across the left hand corner of their paper; the envelopes however being plain.   One's address in raised blue letters at the top of the sheet is in good taste.   The address and date should always be placed either at the beginning or the end of a letter.   In notes, the date and address usually appear at the end.   In dating a letter, the day of the month and the year are given, thus, "February 14, 18—"   It is sufficient on a note to give the day of the week.

FOLDING, SEALING AND STAMPING LETTERS.

Some people have very slovenly habits in the folding, addressing and the stamping of their letters.   In all cases the sheet should be neatly folded and so placed in the envelope that, when removed by the recipient, it will open out right side up—that is, so it may be read without turning.   The stamp must always be placed evenly at the upper right-hand corner of the envelope.   To put it anywhere else is not allowable, and to turn it upside down, sidewise, or diagonally shows carelessness and want of taste.   Stamped envelopes are allowable only for business communications.   The old fashion of sealing letters with wax is again in favor, but it should be adopted only by those who have learned how to make a clean, even, clearly marked seal.   A slovenly seal is intolerable.

A QUESTIONABLE IMPROVEMENT.

The new style of writing on the first and fourth sides of a sheet, then opening it out and writing across the second and third sides continuously, is a very doubtful one and rather to be avoided than copied.   The old natural way of

writing on the pages of the sheet in their order is certainly
more sensible.

USE BLACK INK.

Purple ink was in great favor some years ago but is
no longer so. Plain black is now preferred by persons of
taste, and, like good white paper, it is really always in
fashion. Of course none but country lads and lasses evei
use red or blue inks.

WRITING NOTES.

In writing notes careful discrimination should be exercised both as to matter and manner. A familiar note
should be answered in like tone; the ceremonious note
should be acknowledged ceremoniously. As suggested elsewhere the confusion of the first and third persons is a great
and common error. It should be studiously avoided.

HOW TO BEGIN A LETTER.

How shall a letter be begun? Shall we begin with "My
Dear Mr. Jones," or simply "Dear Mr. Jones?" Is the first
or the last form the more familiar? As ordinary custom in
this country has sanctioned the former as the usual way of
beginning a letter, it is argued that where the "my" is
dropped, the "Dear Mr. Jones" becomes more familiar than
the other form. But "Dear Sir," or "Dear Madam," following the name of the person addressed, .may be substituted. An unmarried lady is not permitted, according to an
English authority, to address a gentlemen as "My Dear
Sir." She may do no more than write "Dear Sir." To
write "Dear Miss" is very awkward. It were better to

write it "Dear Miss Brown" or "My Dear Miss Green." In writing formally to a clergyman the letter should be begun thus: "Reverend and Dear Sir." Among intimate friends forms of address are used to suit themselves.

THE CLOSING OF A LETTER.

Letters of a formal character should be closed with some formal expression, as "Your obedient servant." "Yours truly," "Yours very truly," and "Yours respectfully," are reserved for business letters. "Cordially yours," "Faithfully yours," "Affectionately yours," are familiar forms for use in friendly correspondence, but ingenious people will frame a new set of words for every occasion, fitting them, as Wilkins Micawber was wont to do, to the state of his mind or to the object of his letter.

NEATNESS.

Great care should be taken to avoid blotting and blurring. It is neither a compliment to your correspondent nor to yourself to send a letter or note marred by splotches and blurr of ink. It is also inexcusable to cross your lines, as if stingy of paper as well as indifferent to the eyes of the one to whom you write. The whole sheet may be filled, if desired, but criss-crossing must never be indulged.

UNDERSCORING.

Underscoring is often carried to an absurd excess, especially by very young ladies, who italicize every other word and thus rob their emphasis of all real significance. No word should be underscored unless its importance is very great.

A Scrap of a Letter.

MOURNING PAPERS.

Real grief is always unostentatious, hence mourning papers with exaggerated borders of black are in extreme bad taste.

ENCLOSING STAMPS.

Stamps should be enclosed to pay the return postage on manuscript sent to a publisher. You should also enclose a stamp when writing on a business matter that concerned yourself alone. Never enclose postage when writing to a friend. Be sure that you put on stamps enough to fully prepay the postage on your letters.

NEVER DISPLAY ILL-TEMPER IN A LETTER.

It is never wise to make a display of ill-temper, and it is especially unwise to make such a display in a letter, which may be preserved and rise up to plague you. If you feel that you must give vent to your passion, do so; but lay your letter aside till next day, when, your temper having cooled, you will probably be ashamed of yourself and throw what you had written in the fire. In other words, be civil in your correspondence as in your direct personal intercourse. High words will not add strength to a weak cause, but they will often weaken a strong cause and detract from the dignity of the man or woman who employs them.

EVERY LETTER SHOULD BE ANSWERED.

It is laid down as a rule that every letter should be answered, no matter who the writer may be. If the letter be impertinent, acknowledge its receipt just the same; you can check further impertinence by the tone of your answer, which, however pointed, must be polite.

NEVER USE SCRAPS OF PAPER.

Writing on scraps of paper is not to be encouraged. If your correspondence is worth anything it is certainly worth a full sheet of good paper.

ADDITIONAL HINTS.

Avoid the first person singular as much as possible, and in writing letters, on business especially, be brief. Go right to the heart of the subject without circumlocution, and do not bring in any extraneous matter. In writing to friends spare them the details of your trials and tribulations. They probably have enough of their own without being troubled with your personal affairs. A letter, like a visit, should be bright and cheerful; and a correspondent has no more right to be disagreeable than a guest.

Never send an anonymous letter. Nothing is more cowardly and abominable, and one who is known to resort to such a means of effecting his ends is very properly detested by all right-minded people.

INVITATIONS.

INVITATIONS.

The etiquette of invitations is full of nice details that society insists that its votaries shall closely observe and strictly follow. An invitation must not only be properly worded, addressed and sent—it must be properly acknowledged; and any slip from the accepted form on either side is held as a sort of social misdemeanor worthy of severe reprehension. It is the purpose of this chapter to present the usages in this connection so plainly that the wayfaring man though a fool need not err therein.

IN WHOSE NAME TO ISSUE INVITATIONS.

All invitations, save those to a dinner, are issued in the name of the lady of the house. Dinner invitations are issued in the names of both the host and hostess, except where the dinner is to gentlemen only, when the invitation is in the name of the host alone.

ANSWERING INVITATIONS.

Answers to such invitations must be immediately returned and they must be either accepted or declined unequivocally. You must not condition an acceptance on your presence in town, or your recovery from an illness, or the conclusion of a business engagement. If you have the slightest doubt of your ability to be present on the occasion, your declination must be peremptory. To leave the success of an entertainment depending on contingencies ,beyond the knowledge or control of the host and hostess is inexcusable. Your answer should invariably be addressed to the person or persons issuing the invitation. If the invitation comes from Mr. and. Mrs. Brown, your answer must be addressed to Mr. and Mrs Brown. If it is in the name of Mr. Brown alone or Mrs Brown alone, then you address ycur answer accordingly.

KEEPING THE ENGAGEMENT.

An invitation once accepted you are under obligation to fulfill the engagement and must do so even at a sacrifice. But if illness should befall, or any other sufficient cause interfere with your attendance, you are bound to send a note immediately to the hostess apprizing her of the fact, so that your place may be filled. For balls and large parties, however, this is not necessary.

WHEN FATHER ENTERTAINS FOR DAUGHTER, ETC.

Where a father entertains for his daughters, as in the case of a widower, his name alone appears in a wedding invitation. But where his eldest daughter presides over the household, invitations to dinners, receptions, etc., are given in both his name and hers. A young lady who is not too young may issue cards to a tea in her own name, if she be at the head of her father's household. Very young ladies are never expected to issue invitations to gentlemen in their own names.

INVITATIONS TO "AT HOMES."

"Balls" are not supposed to be held in private houses. They are always considered public affairs, and so a lady never invites her friends to a "ball" at her own house.   Her invitation will merely announce her "At Home," with "cotillion" or "dancing" in one corner, the date and hour, of course, being given.   Where the affairs are to be small and informal the word "Informal" should appear in one corner.   Gentlemen are never "At Home."   When they issue invitations they "request the pleasure" or "the honor of your company."   Committees also "request the pleasure of your company."

FORMS OF INVITATIONS.

The styles in stationery for invitations, etc., are constantly changing, but severe plainness and simplicity are always in good taste.   Engraved cards and note paper are now quite popular, both by reason of their elegance and their convenience.   Dinner invitations, however, except in large and ceremonious affairs, are often written, and the first person may be used.   Ordinarily the third person is insisted upon in formal invitations and much care should be taken not to mix the persons, as is done where "Mrs. John Smith requests the pleasure of *your* company."   The proper form is: "Mrs. John Smith requests the pleasure of the company of Mr. and Mrs. Thomas Brown;" but in the case of engraved invitations the mixing of the persons is justified on the ground of convenience, since it saves the printing in of names.   Correct forms of all kinds of invitations, acceptances and regrets will be found elsewhere.

INVITATIONS TWO WEEKS IN ADVANCE.

Invitations to formal affairs should be sent out two weeks in advance. Less ceremonious dinners, parties, etc., are signified by the shorter notice; yet the rule is not infallible. The exact character of the affair should be clearly designated in the invitation, so that the recipients may be in no sort of doubt as to whether it is to be ceremonious or informal, a dance or a dinner.

WHEN INVITATION MUST INCLUDE HUSBAND AND WIFE.

Husband and wife must always be included in invitations to affairs in which both sexes are to participate. To invite only one of a married pair would be to insult both, even where it is known that one or the other never goes into society. But as all rules, even social, have their exceptions, so is this one, which is waived sometimes among intimate friends, especially on informal occasions, or where a vacant seat at dinner is to be filled on sudden notice.

HOW TO SEND INVITATIONS.

In this country the sending of invitations by mail has been rather severely discountenanced and ultra-fashionable society has never quite reconciled itself to a means of communication so democratic, preferring special messengers, however untrustworthy, for the service. In England, on the contrary, the public post is considered quite good enough for the aristocrats who send and acknowledge invitations; and even in this country the custom of using the mails for this purpose is said to be growing in favor.

STATIONERY.

Unruled paper is prescribed for all communications other than those of a business character. Hence, invitations, acceptances, regrets and the like are always written on plain sheets, usually note size, either white or toned, according to the fashion. Plain envelopes are also used. The fashion in these things is always ascertainable at a first-class stationer's.

REPLYING TO INVITATIONS.

In accepting an invitation mention the date and hour, so any mistake on that score may be avoided. If you cannot accept, you should give your reason why in plain terms, as "a previous engagement," "absence from the city," "illness in the family," etc. Simply to decline without explanation would leave large room for unpleasant speculation.

It is not allowable to "decline" an invitation. You "regret that a previous engagement prevents you from accepting"—which is the more courteous form. The choice of words in such cases is a very nice one and great care should be exercised lest you employ a form or a phrase that may strike unpleasantly. Abbreviations are not permitted in acceptances or regrets, and in general form they should correspond with the invitation.

No answer is necessary when a lady sends her visiting card with "At Home" and the day and hour written upon it. In acknowledging such an invitation, you send your card, but you are not to write "regrets" or anything else upon it, as that would be considered impolite.

INVITATIONS TO PERSONS IN MOURNING.

Persons in mourning may be invited as a matter of compliment, although it is known that they cannot accept. Their answers to an invitation simply express regrets and nothing more. On the day of the event they mail their visiting cards black-bordered, enclosed in two envelopes, the cards thus serving instead of a personal visit and explaining the declination. The same number of cards should be sent as if one were calling in person; the lady would send one card, and her husband two—one for the host and the other for the hostess.

INVITATION TO MEMBERS OF A LARGE FAMILY.

Where invitations are sent to families containing several members, the approved method is to send one to the husband and wife, another to the daughters, addressed to the Misses Fogg, and a third to the sons, addressed to the Messrs. Fogg. It is not considered good form to send an invitation to "Dr. Squills and family," and it is equally bad form to send a separate invitation to each member of a large household.

ADDITIONAL NOTES.

Caution and good judgment should be exercised in asking for invitations to a ball for friends. It is frequently the case that a hostess has a larger list than she can fill, so that it but adds to her embarrassment if you request her to include others on your account. An invitation may be requested for a distinguished stranger or for a dancing man, if unexceptionable; but rarely for a married pair and almost never for a couple living in the same city, unless they be recent arrivals.

Invitations must always be directed to the private residence and not to the place of business of the person favored.

Verbal invitations are given only where the occasion is very informal, and such invitations imply plain dress. early hours and a small company.

DRESS.

From little matters let us pass to less,
And lightly touch the mysteries of dress;
The outward forms the inner man reveal,
We guess the pulp before we eat the peel.
One single precept might the whole condense—
Be sure your tailor is a man of sense;
But add a little care, or decent pride,
And always err upon the sober side.

—O. W. Holmes.

DRESS.

The question of dress is one that engages a large share of feminine attention, and even the opposite sex is not indifferent to good clothes. ·Men and women alike find an interest in appearing well; and few of either sex wholly neglect those details of the toilet so essential to good taste and personal attractiveness. The outward garb is usually indicative of the inward personality of the wearer; · and our first impressions of those we casually meet are more often formed on the fit of their clothes and their manner of wearing them than upon anything they do or say. Indeed, very little beyond the dress is remarked or remembered after a passing encounter with strangers.

With ladies, however, dress and the toilet in general are of first importance. We hold them to stricter account in these particulars (as in others) than we do men; and women naturally devote more of thought, ingenuity and time to personal attire and adornment than those of the sterner sex whose business absorbs an increasing proportion of their lives and energies.

THE BATH.

Cleanliness, being next to godliness, is, of course, a prime requisite. Fastidiousness in this regard is hardly to be carried too far, yet it is quite possible to be over-nice and therefore disagreeable. The hands, the face, the neck, the arms and, in fact, the whole person must be kept scrupulously clean; but it must not be forgotten that the bath hath its dangers as well as its benefits. To bathe too often may be even worse than not to bathe at all, vitality often being sapped by over-indulgence in the lavatory. Very robust people may perhaps safely bathe twice a day in summer and once a day in winter. One of a weakly constitution should not venture to bathe oftener than once or twice a week. Only those of the hardiest constitutions should take cold shower baths. For ordinary people the sponge bath is the safest as well as the most convenient, tepid water being better than hot or cold, as it cleanses and invigorates at the same time. One should not remain in the bath longer thant hree or four minutes and, if the water be cold, the head should be wet on top before entering.

THE TEETH.

The teeth need much care, but they should not be cleansed with a stiff brush. In order to preserve the teeth very hot and very sweet things must be avoided; and after eating the mouth should be rinsed out thoroughly.

THE HANDS.

The finger-nails require nice attention. They must be kept clean and neatly trimmed, nothing looking worse than long nails, especially if dirty. A liberal use of the nail brush is advised, but all will be in vain if gloves are not worn outdoors and as much indoors as possible.

Among the Flowers.

THE HAIR.

A clean hair-brush is very necessary in the care of one's hair. Hence that instrument of the toilet should frequently be washed in hot water and soda. The hair needs careful brushing both night and morning; and occasionally it should be cleansed with the yolk of an egg beaten, or with a mixture of lime juice and glycerine. Hair tonics and quack washes and the like, as well as dyes, must be let severely alone. Pomades and oils should also be avoided, except in rare instances.

Dyed hair, or hair changed in any way from its natural color, is in the worst taste possible. Color so obtained cannot be otherwise than inharmonious with the skin, the eyes and the eye-brows; and it is not unnaturally regarded with supreme disfavor by people of genuine breeding.

THE COMPLEXION.

A good complexion cannot be had by artificial means. Paints, powders and lotions are all in vain; they merely destroy what little nature may have done for those who use them. A regular diet, with plenty of exercise, and ordinary care in other respects, are the prime requisites for a fine complexion. Early hours are also of great importance, the all-night dance being destructive of health and therefore of that fairness and tone of the skin so essential to beauty. Nor should the face be washed when overheated. First wipe away the perspiration carefully and afterward lave the face in soft warm water, drying with a towel not too harsh

THE ATTIRE.

So much for the care of the person. And now as to its proper adornment, of which so much might be said had we the space at command. We dwelt first upon the care of the person, because really that is of the first importance. For no matter how rich a lady's attire may be, if her fingers show neglect, if her hair be untidy, if there is a suggestion in her appearance of the need of soap and water, all her finery goes for nothing. And even the coarsest is presentable if worn by one who is perfectly clean and tidy.

AVOID EXTREMES.

Fashions in dress change with the times; but through them all there runs a common sense which endures. Extremes are always in execrable taste and must be avoided. Harmony of color as well as of design must be studied and exaggerations of style, either in simplicity or the reverse, are never to be affected. Originality in dress is certainly desirable, but it must stop short of peculiarity. Women no longer young need to be careful in choosing colors. The quieter these are the less likely they will be to attract unfavorable notice to the wearers. Ladies not rich may always appear to advantage if good taste is exercised. Tawdy stuffs are intolerable, but even common fabrics may be made up so skillfully as to look attractive.

SELECTING MATERIALS.

A recent authority on dress gives this wholesome advice: "One should be careful to select materials and styles of dress that are suited to one's age, figure, height and complexion. A great many women consider only the beauty or ugliness of a garment in itself, and quite forget that the same costume will make one woman look like a scare-crow and another like a goddess. They see in the street, perhaps, some "love of a bonnet" worn by a charming young girl with fresh bright complexion, and are filled with a desire and determination to have one just exactly like it, never stopping to think whether it will be equally suitable to a person of a totally different coloring, age and figure."

AVOID TRYING CONTRASTS IN COLORS.

Women are also lacking in discretion in another important particular. They frequently make the most trying contrasts in the quality of separate garments, wearing a showy hat with a plain dress, or a rich cloak over a gown not only old but cheap. This is something particularly to be avoided. Such sharp contrasts are actually painful. It is equally painful to have sharp contrasts in color. There ought to be a certain harmony in every detail of a costume. Failing that it fails in that æsthetic quality which is, after all, the most important.

NEATNESS AND ELEGANCE.

"Neatness and simple elegance," says one writer on dress, "should always characterize a lady, and after that she may be as expensive as she pleases, if only at the right time. And we may say that here simplicity and plainness characterize many a rich woman in a high place; and one can always tell a real lady from an imitation one by her style of dress. Vulgarity is readily seen even under a costly garment,

There should be harmony and fitness, and suitability as to age and times and seasons. Every one can afford vulgarity and slovenliness; and in these days, when the fashions travel by telegraph, one can be *a la mode*."

THE LOW-NECKED DRESS.

The low-necked dress is a fatal lure to many a woman who ought to know better than to display her physical imperfections to the gaze of a pitiless world. Either a fat old woman or a scrawny young one should be wise enough to court the favoring and softening influences of high necks and any other devices for lessening the obviousness of their defects of form.

PLAIN SATINS AND VELVETS, ETC.

Plain satins and velvets and rich dark brocades, if properly made up, are becoming to any one. It is the fashionable colors—the latest thing out—that so often tempt women to violate all the canons of good taste in the matter of dress.

LACING.

Tight-lacing is an abomination in the sight of angels and men. It not only sacrifices health, but it deforms nature, and no deformity can be lovely. Why women will truss themselves up, as many do, is one of the mysteries past finding out. They thus destroy their own comfort and take on a stiffness which makes grace as impossible to them as to a saw-horse.

STUDY HARMONY OF COLORS.

A study in the harmony of colors is one that every

woman ought to make. A mixture of blue and yellow in a costume is something that none but a back-country girl might be expected to venture upon, yet we sometimes find our eyes offended by such a combination by women who assume to be exponents of fashion. Similarly, we should expect only ladies of color to trick themselves out in blue, yet many brunettes in the high social swim set one's teeth on edge by wearing a color that only one with golden hair and fair complexion should choose.

Light brown hair also requires blue, but black hair should be set off by scarlet, orange or white. One with reddish hair may tone it down with scarlet. Where the hair is a golden red, blue, green, purple or black will look well. One with a fair, delicate complexion should wear delicate tints, such as pea-green, light blue and mauve. Where the hair is without natural richness it may be livened up by a judicious choice of colors. A pale yellowish green, for instance, by reflection will produce the lacking warmth of tone. Where one has no eye for color, there is all the more reason for caution. Such a person should consult the judgment of a friend in choosing colors, having a care always that the friend's eye shall not be as dead as her own to harmony.

WASHINGTON ETIQUETTE.

WASHINGTON ETIQUETTE.

The etiquette of the national capital is not exactly the same as that observed elsewhere. It is less democratic, more formal and perhaps less worthy of general imitation than that prevailing in ordinary society. When Thomas Jefferson was president of the United States he introduced an era of simplicity at the capital that was in striking contrast with the courtly manners and forms which were established under the presidency of Gen. Washington, and since Jefferson's time there has never been that aping of royalty by the executive or his subordinates that had previously been observed. Yet Washington social forms still preserve many of the old ideas of caste and precedence, and the president and his official household are hedged about with conventionalities suggestive of a royal court.

PRESIDENT AND FAMILY.

For example, the president and his family neither make nor return calls. They are at the head of official society and their lead is religiously followed. The social season is opened by the White House reception, ending, of course with the beginning of Lent.

WASHINGTON SOCIETY.

Washington society is composed of three classes. First, there is the official class, with the president at its head. It includes all officers elected by the people or appointed by the president in the three branches of the government, as well as the officials appointed by the executive in the various departments, with the members of their families. This includes officers of the army and navy and the marine corps; government officials holding places in the different states of the union, and officers of the diplomatic and consular services of the United States who may happen to be at the capital.

The second class includes members of the diplomatic and consular services of foreign countries, officers of foreign governments, and of officers of state or municipal governments of the United States who may be in the city.

The third class comprises visitors of other places whose social position at home entitles them to recognition, and permanent residents—that is, either those who are rich or occupy high professional or business positions. The department clerks and their families have no recognized social standing.

OFFICIAL RANK.

Official rank is established in the following order, partly by constitutional recognition, partly by law and partly by usage :

The president.

The vice-president, or, when the office of vice-president is vacant, the president of the senate *pro tempore*.

The chief justice of the United States.

Senators.

The speaker of the House.

Representatives in Congress.

Associate justices of the United States.

Members of the cabinet in the order of their succession to the presidency as established by law, as follows:

The secretary of state.

The secretary of the treasury.

The secretary of war.

The attorney general.

The postmaster general.

The secretary of the navy.

The secretary of the interior.

Members of the foreign diplomatic corps.

The general of the army and the admiral of the navy.

The governors of states.

The justices of the court of claims.

Circuit and district judges of the United States.

Chief justices and associates of the territories and the District of Columbia.

The lieutenant-general and vice-admiral.

Major-generals, rear admirals and officers of the staff of equal rank.

Brigadier-generals and commodores, chiefs of semi-independent civil bureaus, chiefs of department bureaus in the order of their chief officers.

Colonels of the navy, staff officers of equal rank, the colonel of the marine corps.

Consuls-general and consuls of foreign governments, and the same of the United States.

Lieutenant-colonels and majors of the army, and commanders and lieutenant-commanders of the navy, and staff officers of equal rank.

The commissioners of the District of Columbia, governors of territories and lieutenants of the army and navy.

Captains, first and second lieutenants of the army, lieutenants, masters and ensigns of the navy, and staff officers of equal rank.

Assistant secretaries of executive department, secretaries of legation, secretaries of the Senate and House, and clerk of the supreme court.

The wives of persons holding these various official positions take precedence with their husbands.

OFFICIAL CALLS.

It was said in another place that the president never returns calls, but there is an exception to be noted. He returns the call of a sovereign, president or ruler of an independent state, but these invariably pay the first visit. The vice-president and members of the senate receive first calls from the associate justices of the supreme court of the United States, the members of the cabinet, the foreign ministers and others below them. The rule also applies to their families.

Members of the House call first upon all persons in the higher grades. The speaker of the House does the same.

The associate justices of the supreme court receive the first call from all officers except the president, vice-president and members of the Senate.

Foreign ministers pay the first call to the secretary of

state and other members of the cabinet, but the first call on families of foreign ministers is made by the families of the cabinet officers.

Strangers of distinction visiting the capital make the first call on resident officials of the same rank. Strangers arriving in Washington should pay the first call and leave a card, and this visit should be returned within a couple of days. This applies as well to social as to official visits.

Newly appointed officials of whatever grade pay the first visit to those above them, receiving the first call from those below.

With the exception noted in the case of calls on the families of foreign ministers, these regulations in regard to calls of ceremony paid by officials apply to the ladies of their families.

RECEPTION DAYS.

Reception days are set apart by the wives of prominent officials and other ladies of high social position. These receptions are very democratic in character. Invitations are not issued, and anybody of reputable fame and suitably dressed may attend. Gentlemen may go either with or without ladies. It is optional with the host whether he makes his appearance. The usual hours for these receptions are from 3 to 6 P. M. Following are the days as they have been allotted by custom to the wives of the various officials:

Mondays, the wives of the justices of the supreme court and the ladies of Capitol Hill.

Tuesdays, the families of the speaker of the House and

the representatives in Congress; also, of the general of the army.

Wednesdays, the families of cabinet officers.

Thursdays, the families of the vice-president and members of the senate.

Fridays, ladies not included in the official circle.

Saturdays, the mistress of the White House.

ETIQUETTE OF RECEPTIONS.

The etiquette of these receptions is quite simple. On arriving you hand your card to the usher, if there be one, and he announces your name. In the absence of that functionary, you drop your card in the receiver in the hall, enter the reception-room, and, if unknown to the lady of the house, pronounce your own name in a distinct voice. After exchanging the usual civilities, pass on to make way for other callers. Refreshments are generally provided at these afternoon receptions and guests are expected to pass almost immediately from the drawing-room, to the dining-room, but haste in this, of course, is to be avoided, as must the appearance of eating a substantial meal, once in the room where the refreshments are served. It is enough to taste a bit of salad, drink a cup of tea or eat an ice. When departing, take leave of the hostess.

Gentlemen on such occasions wear frock coats, light-colored trousers, tan-colored gloves and quiet ties. They may keep their hats in hand, but they must leave their overcoats in the hall. Street costumes are worn by the ladies. The evening receptions in Washington do not materially differ from evening receptions held elsewhere, and the same general rules govern.

THE WHITE HOUSE.

The Saturday afternoon receptions given by the lady of the White House are more especially intended for ladies, but men are not barred. The dress is the same as that for the afternoon receptions of the ladies of the cabinet. The etiquette is the same as that observed at the president's evening receptions, which are held on Thursdays from 8 to 11 P. M. To these no invitations are sent, any one in suitable attire being admitted. Full dress is not essential, though usual, the rule being relaxed in favor of travelers, who may appear in any dark dress, the ladies without bonnets.

On reaching the entrance of the White House, ladies are shown to the cloak-rooms, where they receive checks for their wraps, after which they join the throng and pass on to the reception-room. Each person should mention his own name and that of the lady who accompanies him to the official who makes the introductions to the president. This functionary, usually the marshal of the District of Columbia or the engineer of the public buildings, then presents the gentlemen to the president, and the former, after shaking hands, presents the lady he is escorting, then both pass on to the lady who is receiving, who stands at the president's right. An official stands ready to present the couple. The lady may either bow or shake hands, but the gentleman merely bows. They then pass on immediately, conversation being strictly barred by the exigencies of the situation. Visitors may remain in the White

House as long as they choose, and they are not expected to make their farewells to the president and his wife.

Business calls on the president may be made at the executive office at proper hours. The visitor on being shown to the president's ante-room will hand his card to the official in attendance, who will deliver it at the proper time. Meanwhile the visitor will take a seat and await the pleasure of the president, who may not be able to see him that day. If the caller has no business with the president, but merely wishes to pay his respects, the fact should be indicated on the visitor's card. This will ensure the earliest reception possible. When admitted to the president's office, the visitor should mention his name and residence, and, after bowing and shaking hands, should say a few words and give way to others. Where there is a party together, the first to enter should introduce the others.

SOCIAL ETIQUETTE UNDER PRESIDENT JEFFERSON.

It may be interesting in this connection to reproduce the form of social etiquette prepared by Mr. Jefferson and observed at the capital in early days. It was as follows:

"I. In order to bring the members of society together in the first instance, the custom of the country has established that residents shall pay the first visit to strangers, and, among strangers, first-comers to latter-comers, foreign and domestic; the character of stranger ceasing after the first visits. To this rule there is a single exception. Foreign ministers from the necessity of making themselves known, pay the first visit to the ministers of the nation, which is returned.

"II. When brought together in society, all are perfectly equal, whether foreign or domestic, titled or untitled, in or out of office.

"All other observances are but exemplifications of these two principles.

"I. 1st. The families of foreign ministers, arriving at the seat of government, receive the first visit from those of national ministers, as from all other residents.

"2. Members of the legislature and the judiciary, independent of their offices, have a right as strangers to receive the first visit.

"II. 1st. No title being admitted here, those of the foreigners give no precedence.

"2d. Differences of grade among the diplomatic members gives no precedence.

"3d. At public ceremonies, to which the government invites the presence of foreign ministers and their families, a convenient seat or station will be provided for them, with any other strangers invited and the families of the national ministers, each taking place as they arrive, and without any precedence.

"4th. To maintain the principle of equality, or of *pela mela*, and prevent the growth of precedence out of courtesy, the members of the executive will practice at their own houses, and recommend an adherence to the ancient usage of the country, of the gentlemen in mass giving precedence to the ladies in mass, in passing from one apartment where they are assembled into another."

21

STATIONERY.

Mr. and Mrs. Williams
ask the favor of your
presence at the marriage of their daughter

Nellie

to

Mr. James K. Wilson,

Wednesday, June the Fourth,

at twelve o'clock,

Church of the Redeemer,

Mulberry street.

———

Doctor & Mrs. Smith

request the pleasure of your presence at

the marriage of their daughter

Gladys

to

Mr. Phillip Monroe,

on

Thursday, December Sixteenth,

at eight o'clock,

Euclid Avenue and Thirteenth street.

———

Mr. & Mrs. De Witt Clinton
have the honor of announcing the
marriage of their niece,

Julia,

to

Mr. Henry Lloyd Jones,
in New Orleans,
February Tenth, Eighteen Hundred
and Ninety-Two.
5340 Grand Boulevard.

ANNOUNCEMENT OF MARRIAGE.
331

Mr. and Mrs. Williams

request the pleasure of

Mr. and Mrs. Granger's

Company at Dinner,

On Thursday, January eighth,

at eight o'clock,

112 Walnut Hills Boulevard.

———

FORMAL INVITATION TO DINNER.

1307 Emerald Avenue.

My Dear Mrs. Julian:

Will you and Mr. Julian give us the pleasure of your company at dinner, on Tuesday, October fifteenth, at half-past seven o'clock?

Sincerely yours,

Jennie Fiske.

October sixth.

212 Maryland Street.

Dear Mrs. Brown:

I am very sorry I cannot have the pleasure of dining with you on the 19th to meet Mr. Darlington, as I am going out of town on Monday to be absent a fortnight.

With kindest regards, believe me,

Yours sincerely,

C. E. Craddock.

3940 Wymore Avenue.

Mr. and Mrs. Vandyke
have much pleasure in accepting
Mr. and Mrs. Silverlea's
kind invitation to dinner on Thursday,
September the tenth, at eight o'clock.

August 20.

FORMAL ACCEPTANCE, DINNER INVITATION.

ENGRAVED CARD.—AN INVITATION TO TEA.

BLANK CARD FOR DINNER INVITATION.

336

Mr. and Mrs. Lovejoy
request the pleasure of
Mr. and Mrs. Cameron's
Company on Tuesday Evening, Jan-
uary ninth, at seven o'clock,
to meet
Henry Carey Bayard.
212 96th St.   *Theatre Party.*

INVITATION TO THEATRE PARTY.

Mr. and Mrs. Howe
request the pleasure of

—

Company at Breakfast,
on Monday, Oct. 11,
at one o'clock.

INVITATION TO BREAKFAST.

Mrs. J. P. Osgood,
At Home
On Thursday, February Ninth.
97 Dayton Avenue.
Music at 4:30 o'clock.

INVITATION TO MUSICALE.

Mr. and Mrs. Devanon
At Home
Monday Evening, March Sixth,
at nine o'clock.
No. 4 Nineteenth Street.
Small Dance.

INVITATION TO SMALL DANCE.

ARCHIBALD GRAY.

THEODORE SYLVANUS ORTON.

DEXTER CLUB.

HAMILTON WILLIAMS.

247 EUCLID AVENUE.

PRESENT STYLE IN CARDS.

Mr. & Mrs. Barry Glyndon.

26 Bryant Terrace..

Mrs. Henry D. Howells.

271 Exeter Court.

Miss Julia Henderson.

24 PARK ROW.

PRESENT STYLE IN CARDS.